Psycho Cage

JUDE LUCAS

SIMPATICO PUBLISHING

**STORIES WITH SOUL
AND VOLTAGE**

Book Cover by Gail Weiner, designed using Canva.

First UK Edition, 2025

Published by Simpatico Publishing United Kingdom

ISBN – 978-1-0687848-7-3

CONTENTS

WELCOME TO THE CAGE.

Dear Reader,

This book is a live wire.
It doesn't beg for your approval. It doesn't flinch.
Psycho Cage is a scream in the dark—Ethan's fists, Willa's defiance,
Clay's unraveling truth.
These kids aren't broken; they're built wrong on purpose.
Their world is a shattered mirror, and every shard cuts.

Don't expect tidy endings or soft landings.
This isn't a story—it's a reckoning.
If you're here for comfort, turn back now.
If you're here for the ache, the chaos, the pulse of something real—step
inside.
You're already one of us.

Welcome to the cage.
Jude

Ax and Skateboards

The Florida sun's a bastard, scorching the asphalt as Tupac's beats thump through my veins—hair's whipping wild in the wind, Merc purring beneath me like a caged beast ready to claw free. I'm not here for Clay's Douchebag Dad flexing up front or some kid bouncing in back like a yappy mutt. I'm here for axes—Grandpa's voice growls in my skull, rough as gravel, etched from years of smoke and grit: "Men use their hands, Ethan—keeps the demons at bay." Fuck yeah, I feel 'em clawing already, restless under my skin, begging for a release only steel can give.

Bullseye Lodge looms ahead—Mercedes growls to a stop, tires kissing gravel, and Jade strides out, camo hugging his frame tight, serpent ink curling down his neck like a warning carved in flesh. He's all grins, ushering me past glass-walled booths—orange mats slap the floor, wooden targets loom, red-white-blue circles screaming some patriotic bullshit I don't buy. A blonde chick's mid-throw, axe spinning wild—bounces off the wood, arcs back chaotic, nearly clips her skull. She sidesteps, giggling like it's a game. I'd pay cold cash to see that blade split her open, crimson splashing the mat—Willa'd love it, hexing that laugh into a scream, her witchy ass grinning beside me in my head.

Jade shoves an axe into my grip—solid, heavy, the blade whispering under my fingertips like it's alive, humming with promise. I step to the line, left foot forward, right planted firm—eyes lock the target, a bullseye begging to bleed. No hiding it—I'm built for this, every muscle coiled, every nerve sparking. Wrist flicks sharp, axe sails—slams dead center, wood splitting with a wet crack that echoes like a gunshot. Jade's hollering, "That's a bad axe, Ethan!"—throws a fist my way. I bump it, grinning wide, teeth bared—Clay's muttering "asshole" somewhere behind, but he knows he's in my debt. Always will be, the fucker.

Jade's grin stretches, voice dropping low, conspiratorial: "Knife booth's new—where'd you pick that up?" I flip my switchblade, casual, letting it dance between my fingers—he flinches, eyes darting, then slides me a machete, its edge glinting hungry. "Boss'd freak, but try it." I nail a playing card—bullseye, clean through, blade sinking deep—one slip and that steel's in Jade's neck, his grin fading fast as blood would. "Blades are my life," I say, keeping the itch buried, pulsing hot in my gut. "Sixteen?" he asks, sizing me. "Seventeen soon—September," I shrug, tossing my hair. "Swing by summer—knife guys are rare." Instagram swapped, deal sealed—Merc hums me out, that blonde staring as I roll, her eyes hooked. Kayla'd scoff—cheerleaders can't throw for shit—but she'd beg me to teach her, that pout working overtime, lips promising trouble I'd take.

Mom's spaghetti sauce simmers thick, pulling me back from the axe-throwing high as I slouch at the dinner table—David's stuffing his face, meatball dripping red down his chin, barking about some dead-end job he'll shove me into—"Duffney Street's slow, Ethan—won't fuck it up too bad," he laughs, swigging beer. Brent's glued to his phone across from me—two years older, my shadow, but I'm the king here—his eyes flicker up, catching mine before darting back down. Baby Kacey's in her highchair, flinging nuggets like grenades—I swat 'em mid-air, smirking—"Nice try, kid." Mom hovers, piling more into my bowl like I'm five—her second glass of wine trembles in her hand, a far cry from the Oxy cocktails she drowned in before David's cash cleaned her up—almost.

I scoop the pasta, fork twisting fast—David's still yapping—"Business someday, kid"—but I tune him out, my phone buzzing hot in my pocket. Willa's text lights the screen—"Come over, E"—her witchy pull yanks me, and I'm already half gone. Mom nudges me—"Talk to your dad"—but I shove the phone down, ignoring her—Brent smirks, knowing I'm out. I snatch my skateboard, the door slamming behind me—David's "Where the fuck—" cuts off as I roll into the humid night, the air thick with mowed lawns and palm trees whispering boredom.

The neighborhood stretches out, a copy-paste prison—fancy cars gleam in driveways, hedges clipped too perfect, white houses glaring under streetlights like they're hiding something rotten. Mrs. Kelly waves from her yard, fussing over roses—I flip her an Ollie, grinning as she gasps. Mr. Gadding buffs his ride, yelling—"Slow down, punk!"—but I laugh, wind whipping my hair—fuck his rules. Two girls giggle ahead—short skirts, eyes tracking me—I kickflip smooth, tossing my hair—"Hey, cuties"—they blush, and I'm gone, wheels humming toward Willa's street.

Her house looms—peeling paint, that witchy scent of Palo Santo seeping out—I ring the bell, and she swings the door wide, all black denim and bikini top, jumping into my arms. Her lips crash mine, cherry tang sparking me alive—I'm hers, but I own this too. She grabs my hand, bouncing up the stairs—neighborhood fades, her pull's all I feel—"Ink time, E"—and I'm in, grinning—"Fuck yeah."

Willa drags me up the creaking stairs, her grip tight and warm, denim shorts brushing my hand as we step into her room—the air shifts heavy with Palo Santo and rain-soaked forest, a faint floral curl weaving through like a spell's quiet breath. Candles flicker on a corner table she's turned into an altar—crystals catch the glow for earth, a bell hums soft for air, water rests still in a glass cup, and a red candle spits flame, her core blazing bright. A pentagram sprawls across the center, sage and Palo Santo sticks crisscrossing it—her witchy world pulses alive, drawing me in deep. She's danced with this since we were kids—rose petals and sand back then, now blood and mugwort—and I can't shake the thought she's hexed me, her pull lodged tight in my skull.

I sink onto her bed, the mattress groaning under my weight, and eye the tattoo gear lined up—needles, ink, gloves, all primed like weapons for war. "Upside-down crosses?" I ask with a grin—she slides on gloves, the cool plastic snapping against her skin, and the gun's buzz fills the room like a low, hungry growl. Her fiery red hair tumbles down, framing her face in a rebel halo—winged eyeliner cuts sharp, purple LED glow casting shadows over her cheekbones. "St. Peter's cross," she murmurs, her voice low and dripping with mystery—"he flipped it, didn't deserve Jesus's death." The needle bites my neck just below my earlobe—pain flares, but her touch ignites it—I'm hers in this moment, yet still king of my own chaos.

She flips open a leather-bound book, pages creaking as devil paintings spill out—horned figures with sleek wings—and I lean closer, hooked on the heat of her nearness. "Lucifer's Venus," she whispers, her finger tracing the lines—"morning star, brightness in Hebrew." Our hands brush—hers soft, mine rough—and I pull her in, the spark flaring hot between us. Another page turns—a devil man stares back, fiery hair spilling wild, bloodshot eyes glinting with a single tear—he's me, chained but unbroken. "Rebelled and fell," she says, her voice weaving a hypnotic thread—"steals body and soul—believe in him, E?" I grin—"Fuck yeah"—and yank her closer, lips crashing into hers, cherry tang mixing with her dark hum.

Her skin burns smooth under my mouth—I graze her neck, teeth sinking just enough to draw a gasp, marking her with a bruise that blooms like our own private hex. Sweat slicks us—the Florida heat presses in from outside, her witchy fire blazing here within—she pulls back with a giggle and grabs that devil book, settling against the pillows. Candlelight dances across her face—she's a goddamn goddess flipping through those pages—"He's chained," she murmurs, "but free in me." I'm lost in her—fighter softens for a breath, but my itch holds strong—Willa's mine, and I'm hers, the fresh ink stinging as that upside-down cross brands us both.

I leave Willa's house with her witchy hum still buzzing under my skin as I grab my board and roll out into the night air, thick and humid with Florida's heavy breath of cut grass and salt curling around me. Clay's waiting at the skate park—a text lights my phone, "Library steps, bro"—and I weave through the neighborhood's fake perfection, my wheels humming past white houses and clipped hedges that hide their rot while the wind whips my hair into a tangled mess. I kickflip past

Mrs. Kelly's roses—she gasps like always—and laugh low, speeding toward the concrete ramps glowing under the streetlights' harsh stare.

Clay slouches on the steps with his cap backward, puffing a blunt that trails sweet smoke into the night—he spots me and his grin spreads wide as he calls out, "E, my man!" I drop my board, roll up smooth, and snatch the weed from his fingers, taking a long drag that burns my throat with a sharp, sugary bite before I exhale and grin back—"Fuck yeah, Clayboy." We skate lazy circles under the buzzing lights—ollies and grinds flow easy, our boards clacking against rails as we trade laughs and drags, our friendship carved deep from years of skate scrapes and shared nights stretching out ahead like this one promising trouble.

He pushes hard off the ramp's edge for a kickflip—his board twists mid-air but he lands awkward, his ankle buckling under him as he sprawls across the concrete with a curse spilling loud into the quiet—"Fuck, E, it's twisted bad!" Two girls roll by—tanned legs flashing under short skirts, giggles bubbling up—and they pause, leaning in close as they offer, "Need a lift?" I nod quick—"ER, now"—and we pile into their beat-up hatchback, Clay wincing in the back while I ride shotgun, grinning as the blonde driver floors it through the empty streets. At the ER, Clay hobbles in—a nurse patches him up fast—but my eyes catch the woman beside us, her finger wrapped in a dishtowel that's gone from white to a screaming crimson, tears streaming down her face as she sits in a world of hurt.

"What happened?" I ask, keeping my voice casual though I can't peel my eyes off her—her bloody mess pulls me like a train wreck I don't want to miss. She glances my way, her free hand tidying her hair bun like she's got some pride to hold onto even now, and winces as she fidgets with the towel soaking red. "I was chopping an onion with my new knife and it slipped, I guess," she says, her voice tight with pain—I chuckle low, easing the air—"Must be one hell of a knife—you holding up?" Her mascara leaves tracks on her cheeks as she nods—"It really hurts"—and I lean closer, drawn in—"Mind if I take a peek?" She throws back, "What's your name?"—"Ethan"—and she offers a small, pained smile—"I'm Vanessa."

She flinches as she unwraps the towel, and fuck, it's intense—her finger's nearly hanging off, bone glinting under the blood that drips down her hand and soaks the cloth deeper red. "Fuck, that's serious," I say, my eyes glued to the crimson flow—she shivers, "I need to be more careful around knives," and a nurse guides her away, leaving me staring after her.

Clay's out soon—ankle taped, girls flirting soft—but I'm gone, slipping into the restroom with the lock clicking shut behind me. I lean against the sink—Vanessa's bloody hand floods my head, red dripping, bone stark—my breath catches as I drop my pants, gripping myself tight, stroking hard and fast while the dark rush builds wild and filthy—fuck, it's me, alive in this. I finish quick, panting heavy, smirking into the scratched mirror—"King shit"—then wash up slow and roll back out, Clay none the wiser as the night stays mine to rule.

CROSSES AND CLASSES

I wake up tangled in sheets, the Florida sun slipping through cracked blinds to jab my eyes as last night's weed haze clings thick in my skull—Willa's witchy hum and Vanessa's bloody hand weave into a dark, dirty blur that curls a smirk across my lips. My neck stings where Willa's upside-down cross sits fresh, inked deep below my earlobe—I stretch slow, savoring the ache, when Mom's voice rips through the house like a siren, shrill and furious—"Ethan, get your ass down here now!" I roll out of bed, tugging on yesterday's jeans, and shuffle into the kitchen where Brent's slouched with his phone, smirking sly—he's snitched, I can feel it—and Mom's pacing, her coffee trembling in her hand as Kacey babbles in her highchair, David already gone to the shop.

"What the hell's this tattoo shit Brent's yapping about?" she snaps, slamming the mug down—coffee sloshes over the edge as she storms toward me, grabbing my jaw to tilt my head, her fingers digging in while she stares at the cross like it's a knife in her back. "Upside down—some devil mark? You out of your mind?" I jerk free, grin-

ning—"It's mine, Mom—chill"—but she's unraveling, voice climbing as Brent watches, his snitch ass smug—"You think this is funny?
After all I've been through?" Her past spills out like a flood she can't
hold back—years of running from men and misery, my real dad's fists
smashing her face and my ribs 'til he vanished when I was eight, leaving
us bouncing from trailers to roach holes, her drowning in pills and
cheap gin 'til David's auto shop cash dragged her into this middle-class
maze of clipped lawns and fake smiles.

"You don't get it," she says, her voice breaking as she grips the counter
with knuckles still faintly stained from last night's wine—"I fought
to pull us out, scraped by with nothing while your dad beat us
bloody and left, and David gave us this—and you throw it back with
some punk tattoo?" I laugh low, leaning against the wall—"Saved us?
David's a paycheck, not a savior"—and her eyes flare, hand swinging
fast—she slaps me hard, the sting waking me sharper as Kacey wails
and Brent's smirk fades, his phone dropping silent. "Ungrateful little shit," she hisses, tears brimming—"you're marking yourself like
him?" I rub my jaw, smirking—"Dad's gone—David's nothing—this
is me"—and she turns away, shaking her head as the coffee cools and
Kacey's cries echo through the room.

My phone buzzes—Willa's text glows—"Meet you at locker"—and
I'm half out, snatching my board as Mom's voice chases me—"You'll
ruin us!"—but I let the door slam on her chaos, my neck burning with
that cross—fighter's ink, my own damn crown—rolling free into the
humid morning, her mess a shadow I've already outrun.

I roll up to school on my board, the morning sun already baking the asphalt as Willa's "Meet you at locker" text hums in my
pocket—Mom's screams about the tattoo fade into the buzz of kids

spilling through the halls, their chatter bouncing off chipped lockers like static I tune out. I weave past the crowd—jocks flexing, geeks scurrying—and spot Kayla at her locker, mid-cheer move with her squad, filming a TikTok that's all legs and giggles—her blonde pony-tail swings high, skirt flipping up as she kicks and spins, fuck—my grin twists—every curve catching the light just right. She's a fucking vision—tight top hugging her chest—fuck—my grin twists—curves hit hard—hips swaying like a dare—leaning against the wall, my pulse kicking hard as her laugh rings out, bright and sharp, pulling me in like a moth to her flame.

Maxine's there too—rat-faced, all sneer—hovering at Kayla's elbow with her phone out, filming but glaring my way like I'm trash she'd love to stomp. She's hated me since forever—some petty grudge from middle school I don't give a shit about—and I flash her a grin, slow and dark—"Keep staring, Max"—knowing it'll twist her up tighter. Kayla lands her move, flipping her hair back as the cheer girls squeal—"Perfect, Kay!"—and she catches my eye, tossing a wink that hits like a spark—fuck, she knows what she's doing, those curves a weapon she wields easy. I lick my lips, imagining her close—sweat, glitter, that pout begging for trouble—and my neck stings where Willa's cross sits fresh, a reminder I'm hers too.

Willa's voice cuts through, low and witchy—she's leaning against my locker now, all black denim and that bikini top peeking out, her red hair spilling wild as she slides closer, her eyes narrowing—"What you looking at, E?" I turn slow, smirking—"Just some cheer shit"—but she's not buying it, stepping in 'til her breath brushes my neck, her hand grazing my chest where the tattoo hides under my shirt. "Kayla's ass, huh?" she murmurs, a hex in her tone—I laugh low, pulling her against me—"You're my witch"—and her lips curl, sharp and dangerous—"Better be"—as Kayla's giggle echoes down the hall, Maxine's glare burning holes, and I'm caught between them, king of this fucked-up game.

I slouch into Ms. Jasper's English class, kicking my board against the wall and claiming a desk in the back—fuck the front-row geeks. The hallway buzz still hums in my skull—Kayla's hips swaying past my locker like a tease I'd kill for, Willa's fingers grazing mine with that witchy heat, Maxine's rat-face glare slicing through the crowd like she's plotting my grave. Ms. Jasper's up front, cardigan sleeves shoved up, scribbling *Macbeth: Power & Consequence* on the whiteboard in her prissy little script. She's young—too fucking young—fresh outta college, probably thinks Shakespeare's gonna save our sorry asses.

Willa slinks in beside me, red hair spilling wild over her face as she leans close, her knee jamming into mine like a dare. "Saved your spot, E," she mutters, voice low and dark, dripping hex. Across the room, Kayla's parked with her cheer bitches, Maxine hissing some shit that sets 'em giggling—Kayla flicks her eyes my way, a quick spark, then gone. My neck stings where Willa's upside-down cross bites fresh under my collar—ink's still raw, my crown.\

"Alright, shut it, people," Ms. Jasper snaps, clapping twice like we're fucking dogs. "Macbeth's ambition—where's it drag him?" Pages rustle, kids groan—I spin my pencil between my fingers, letting it dance, fuck the book. "Ethan." Her voice cuts sharp, yanking me outta my head. "You're so into this—gimme your take." I lean back, grinning wide, teeth bared. "Dude offs whoever for power, fucks himself hard. Lady Macbeth's guilt screws him worse than the blood on his hands." My voice roughs the air, daring her. Ms. Jasper's brows twitch up, lips tight. "Crude as hell, but you're not totally off. Who's got more?"

Willa's breath hits my ear, hot and close. "You'd slit throats for less, E—been itching for it since we were brats." It's just for me, her witchy whisper curling in deep. She knows—the blade's been my pulse since I first gripped one, that dark itch I bury from everyone but her.

I sketch a horned devil in the corner of my notebook while Ms. Jasper paces the front of the room, talking about blood and fate. Kayla stretches her legs out under her desk, cheerleader-flexible. I watch, imagining her movements just for me until Willa's shoulder presses against mine. "She's nothing, E," she whispers.

I turn, meeting her dark-lined eyes. "You're my witch." It's low, just between us as the bell rings, cutting Ms. Jasper off mid-sentence. I grab my board, pushing through the door before everyone else, Willa's fingers brushing mine as we exit. Kayla watches us go, Maxine's eyes burning holes in my back. School's just another cage, and I've never been good at staying locked up.

The end of school rolls around, the final bell cutting through the halls like a jailbreak signal—Clay catches my eye across the crowd, and we bolt, ninja-style, slipping through a gap in the metal fence as the woods swallow us whole, their edge hugging the school's concrete sprawl. Golden sunlight filters through the leaves, weaving dreamlike patterns across the ground as we venture deeper—pine needles and damp soil fill the air with a rich, earthy bite that clings to my lungs, pulling me out of the chaos into this peaceful sanctuary where towering trees loom with rough bark draped in soft green moss. Palmetto bushes speckle the forest floor, delicate vines twisting through it all—I lean against a trunk, the humidity slicking my skin as Clay flops beside me, breathing deep while birds sing sweet melodies overhead and leaves rustle like Mother Nature's spinning a private track just for us.

We soak it in 'til the buzz fades, then bounce over to Clay's place, crashing into his room where the digital chaos of *Grand Theft Auto* takes over—time slips away as we sink into the couch, controllers in hand, cracking up and talking trash at the screen while sirens wail and cars explode in pixelated glory. Later, I roll home with the sun dipping low, painting the sky bloody orange—the aroma of a burger wrapped in tinfoil greets me as I step inside, Mom and David's laughter spilling from the living room where they're glued to a *Friends* rerun on the TV. I wave loose—"Hey"—and climb the stairs, my neck still tingling from Willa's ink, the day's heat clinging to my skin.

I jump onto my bed, kick back, and scroll through TikTok—videos flash by as I stuff the burger and chips into my mouth, grease smearing my fingers while I chat with Willa—her text pops up, "wyd?" I grin, typing back—"nothing babe. U?"—and she fires quick—"bn looking up abt Mercury Retrograde. Here watch this"—a YouTube link drops, some astrology spiel I'll skim later. "Thx," I reply, "u know what will really help me during this retrograde?" She hits back—"??"—and I smirk—"A naked picture of you"—her "lol" buzzing back fast as I lean deeper into the pillows, burger gone, waiting for her next move.

Then my phone jolts—a notification from Kayla—and I open it, eyes damn near popping as a private Snap fills the screen—she's posing in her cheerleading skirt, hands cupping her tits, that seductive look piercing straight through me like a dare.

"WTF," I type, "Epic pic but WTF"—her reply flies back—"Omg. I can't believe I sent this to u. It was a mistake"—and I grin—"Great pic tho ;)"—knowing it's no mistake at all. "omg I am so embarrassed," she texts, "and besides, Willa will kill me if she knows"—I shoot back—"I won't tell her ☺ so who was the picture meant for? Ur weed dealer

Jayden?"—and she snaps—"Not funny. Thx for keeping it between us x"—I reply—"np"—and she ends with—"nite"—me tossing—"c u at school."

Her tits linger in my head—full, perfect from what I saw—and I use the memory, hand slipping fast under the sheets, stroking hard 'til the rush hits—dark, wild, king shit—before crashing out, the night swallowing me whole.

PINEAPPLE & CHASERS

Friday night rolls in fast, the football field alive under blazing stadium lights as Clay and I claim a spot on the sidelines—helmets crash and the crowd roars, but my eyes lock on Kayla out there with her cheer squad, flipping and spinning like she owns the turf. Her blonde ponytail swings high with every move—skirt flaring up as she kicks those long, tanned legs skyward, her tight top clinging to curves that hit me like a punch—fuck, she's a wildfire, every twist and bounce pulling my gaze tighter. I lean back on the bleachers, smirking as Clay puffs a vape beside me, the sweet haze curling into the crisp night air while the game blares on, some jock slamming into the endzone—but it's her I watch, her body bending in ways that spark a dark lust creeping up my spine.

"She's mine," I say low, nodding toward Kayla as she lands a perfect flip—Clay exhales slow, grinning—"You wish, bro"—but I don't laugh, my eyes tracing her hips, her ass, the way she moves like she knows I'm here, that wink from the locker still burning in my head. "Watch," I tell him, voice rough—she's out there flipping for the crowd, but it's me she's teasing, her curves a dare I'd kill to claim, and I feel Willa's cross sting my neck, a witchy leash I'll snap when I'm ready. Clay nudges me—"Willa's gonna hex your ass"—and I smirk darker—"Let her try"—imagining Kayla's skin under my hands, her cheer skirt hiked up, that pout begging for trouble while the game fades to noise, tension seeding deep in my gut.

The whistle blows—halftime hits—and Kayla's squad scatters, her eyes flicking my way quick before she turns back to her girls, leaving me hard and restless—Clay vapes again, oblivious, talking some shit about the quarterback, but I'm gone, lost in her fire—lust twisting darker, wilder, a fighter's edge sharpening as I watch her move, knowing she's mine to take, Willa's hex or not.

The football game fades into the night as I slip out past the bleachers—Clay's still buzzing about some play, but Kayla's all I see, her cheer skirt swishing as she breaks from the squad and heads toward the parking lot, her blonde ponytail catching the stadium lights like a beacon pulling me in. I catch up quick, boots crunching gravel—she turns, that pout flashing fast—and I grin, pulling my vape from my pocket as she mirrors me, her own puffing a sweet cloud that mixes with mine in the humid air. "Hey," I say, voice low—she exhales slow, her eyes flicking over me—"Hey, E"—and we lean against some beat-up truck, the metal cool against my back while her warmth hits me closer, her curves a tease I can't shake.

"I hate this fucking place," she says, her rant spilling out as she vapes again—her words tumble fast, sharp with venom—"this school, these people, all of it—fake asses and dumb jocks like Rick thinking they own me." I take a drag, the buzz settling deep—she's hooked me, her fire stoking mine—and I smirk, leaning in—"Rick's a prick—thinks

he's got you?" She laughs, bitter and bright—"He wishes"—and my
gut twists, dark lust creeping up as I imagine him trying, my hands
itching to rip her shirt right here, peel that cheer top off and claim what
he can't. "You're mine," I mutter, half to her, half to the night—her
eyes catch mine, glinting—"Yours, huh?"—and she steps closer, vape
smoke curling between us like a dare.

Her skirt brushes my leg—fuck—my grin curls—rip it off—those hips
sway, her scent hitting me—sweat, glitter, some fruity vape juice—and
I'm fucking hooked, jealousy flaring hotter at Rick's name while my
mind runs wild—shirt torn, her curves bare under my grip, that pout
begging against me. "Fuck this place," she says again, softer now—her
hand grazes mine, sparking heat—and I grin darker—"Fuck 'em
all"—imagining her pressed against this truck, her cheer moves bending just for me, stakes rising as her breath quickens, her eyes daring me to make it real. "You're trouble," she murmurs, vape dangling—my laugh's low, rough—"You've got no idea"—and the night
hums around us, tension thick, blood close.

Willa collected Monster High dolls—I remember it clear as I watch
Kayla now, her skirt brushing my leg while Maxine slinks up, tugging
her arm—back at Cheetham High that first day, fourteen and raw,
I'd rolled in on my board, and Willa found me fast, her black boots
stomping loud, denim clinging tight, red hair spilling wild as she cor-
nered me at my locker. She leaned in close—her voice was low, witchy,
slicing through the hall's buzz—"Stay away from Kayla, E—she's
mine, hands off"—and I grinned, caught by her edge, those dolls she
loved—dark, freaky Monster High girls—stacked on her shelf beside
sage and bones, so different from Kayla's bright American Girl col-
lection with their perfect dresses and rainbow vibes. They weren't the
same—Willa all black, Kayla every pop of color—and fuck, I craved

them both, equal force pulling me hard even then, Willa's warning seeding this triangle that's tightening now.

Kayla's laugh pulls me back—Maxine's dragging her off, whispering shit as they go—and I vape again, watching her hips sway, that snap of her tits still burning in my head—lust twists darker, wilder, a fighter's edge sharpening as I imagine her pressed against this truck, her cheer skirt hiked up, Willa's hex be damned.

Drugs & Jocks

Willa's phone screams—shrill as fuck—ripping me outta sleep, the night thick and sticky around us. My room's a black hole, her witchy heat pressed against me from earlier—vape haze still stinking up the sheets. She jolts up, red hair a wild mess, snatching the buzzing bastard off the floor, her voice dropping low and tight as she listens. Then she's off it fast, eyes flashing like hexed steel—"Kayla and her mom went at it—she's bolted." I grab my phone—4 a.m. burns dim—and she's already yanking her black dress on, boots stomping, urgency sparking her moves—"We're waking Clayboy, he's driving us to Jayden's."

She's rushing now—"Trust Kayla to pull this drama shit"—and I'm up, jeans on, adrenaline kicking as we blow up Clay's phone—five calls, pleading we need to save Kayla from some sketchy dealer 'til he grumbles—"Fine, fuck"—and we're out, the night swallowing us whole.

Clay's heavy foot slams the gas—His dads truck roaring down the highway, headlights cutting through the dark as the engine hums a low growl, tires chewing asphalt while wind whips through the cracked windows, tangling Willa's hair into a wild mess against the leather seat. I lean forward—"This is insane"—and Clay mutters back—"Damn right"—his vape glowing as he puffs, steering us past strip malls and gas stations, their neon signs blurring into streaks of light that fade into the black void beyond. Willa stares out, her jaw tight—"She's at Jayden's"—and I don't ask how she knows, her witchy edge a map I trust—Clay glances over—"How we sure?"—and she mumbles—"If not us or Maxine, it's him—she's got no one else"—her voice trailing into the rumble of the truck as we barrel toward the edge of town.

The vibe shifts hard as we roll into Jayden's sketchy turf—suburban gloss peels away, replaced by potholed roads winding past rundown houses with faded red siding, rusty chain-link fences leaning tired, overgrown yards spilling weeds and junk like ghosts of the shitholes Mom dragged us through before David's cash pulled us out. Clay eases the truck to a stop across from Jayden's crib—the interstate hums faint in the distance, a lone pulse against the stillness as gravel crunches under our boots when we step out, the air thick with damp rot and a hint of burnt sugar. The porch groans under our weight—old furniture sags, a busted lamp flickers, random pipes gleam silver in the dim light—and I grab one, its cold heft solid in my grip as I smirk—"Dude's drug cash could fix this dump." Muffled voices leak from inside—my hold tightens—and Willa knocks, the sound bouncing sharp through the quiet street.

A curtain jolts—Jayden's face peeks out, dirty-blond buzz cut military-tight, then vanishes—commotion stirs—"Aye, Kayla, what them friends want?"—and the door creaks open just enough, his intense blue eyes locking mine through the gap—ink sprawls across his face, stars under one eye, a cross with "hope" and "fear" framing it, "cut here" etched bold on his neck like a dare I'd take. A flame-and-candle tat sits between his brows—not a dick, but fuck, it's wild—girls'd swoon over this bad-boy shit—lean frame in a grimy black tee, silver hoop piercing his brow glinting as he sways, high as hell, red eyes hazy with that hot, reckless edge. "Hey, Willa, what you want?" he slurs, voice thick and slow—she's steady—"Hi, Jayden, we're here for Kayla"—and his gaze shifts, sizing me, Clay, back to her, head shaking sluggish—"She ain't here—ain't seen her in days."

I step up—"Then you won't mind us checking, right?"—and his scowl flares, brows knitting tight—"Listen, fool, I don't know you—I ain't letting strangers in my crib—told you she ain't here, none of your damn business." His eighth-grade Travis Scott drawl almost cracks me up—but he's lean, no muscle under that tee, and I'm bigger, wilder—violence wins— I shove through—head-butting him hard—fuck—blood drips—my grin curls—pain spikes as he sprawls, blood pouring. He drops to the floor, clutching his nose while blood pours through his fingers—his flailing arms miss me, terror flashing in his hazy eyes—and fuck, it feels good, my grin dark as I scan the room—curtains drawn tight, TV flickering *Ancient Aliens* in the corner, sulfur and burnt chemicals choking the air with despair.

Kayla's wedged on the sofa between two burly football jocks—bong smoke curling from one's hand—they stare, stoned or smart, unmoving as Jayden yells—"Help me, bros!"—squirming like a gator on the floor. I ignore him—"Get up, Kayla, we're out"—and she rises, smoothing her pink skirt, the jocks' disappointment etching their ugly mugs as Willa grabs her hand, guiding her past the chaos. I hurl the pipe at the coffee table—glass shatters, wood splinters like fireworks—and Jayden's still down, blood pooling—"I know you, bruh—this ain't over"—but I'm gone, the truck rumbling us away.

The ride home stretches awkward—Kayla and Willa sit stiff, eyes locked out windows, silence heavy as dawn cracks—we drop Kayla off, her mom rushing out with a hug she barely returns—autopilot, distant—her dad shakes my hand firm, Mom's grateful squeeze warm. Kayla sidles close—"You're my hero"—her soft kiss brushes my cheek, stale beer and aftershave lingering as she and Willa vanish inside, leaving me grinning—king of this night.

GIRLS & CARS

S pring break hits full swing, and we're rolling with Clay's Douchebag Dad on a business trip to the city—cruising down Route 1, a podcast blasts through the Merc's speakers, some slick-talking dude droning about unlocking mind power to stack insane cash while I smirk, wondering how much of that bullshit Douchebag Dad needs to peddle his sketchy MLM property schemes to bored housewives desperate for a thrill. Clay leans forward—"Dad, come on, let me take your car while you're in the meeting"—a long shot, but he's swinging hard, and Douchebag Dad chuckles, shaking his head—"You're out of your mind, kid—I ain't letting you handle my Merc in this city—we're parking it and hoofing it—two young bucks like you got energy to burn, so use it." Clay pushes—"But I've got my license, I drive the truck all the time"—and Dad's hand caresses the sports steering wheel like it's his latest fling—"This baby's different"—his voice dripping with pride as he barely lifts a finger to steer, one hand loose on the wheel, the other hanging out the window, flashing that sleeve tattoo like a neon sign.

They're dressed like leopards today—Clay rocks a white shirt with leopard-print shorts, Dad's in a leopard-print shirt, dark jeans, and a gaudy gold cross swinging heavy—every gust of wind through the car smacks me with waves of Aqua Di Gio cologne, sharp and thick, stinging my nose. Dad cranks the podcast louder—"We park, you walk"—his tone final, but Clay's relentless, working angles while the city looms closer—skyscrapers glint against the sun, traffic snarls like a living beast—and by the time we roll in, he's won, Douchebag Dad caving with a grin—"Fine, fetch me later"—double-parking outside a swanky restaurant like he owns the joint, patting the wheel—"Have a blast, boys—don't do anything I wouldn't do." We laugh—he laughs—and Clay slides into the driver's seat, me scrambling from the back to claim shotgun as the engine purrs alive, Clay's Spotify kicking in with Lil Pump's beats flooding the car, pulsing hard as we peel down the street.

People drive like they're in *Grand Theft Auto*—Clay's no exception, weaving through lanes with a mix of skill and reckless hunger, eyes darting for the fastest path as we cruise the sun-soaked beach and bustling harbor strip—music blaring, roof down, turning us into instant douchebags, just like his dad. A group of girls in skimpy shorts and bikini tops strolls by—eyes snag on the flashy Merc, then me—and I tilt my aviator sunglasses, shooting them a wink as we zoom past, their giggles trailing in the wind. This spot's a never-ending party on steroids—car engines roar, horns honk, voices shout over booming beats while waves crash relentless against the shore—the sun beats down, casting a golden glow over sand packed with vivid colors—bright swimsuits, glistening bikinis, bouncing beach balls, soaring frisbees—all shimmering like diamonds on the water.

We roll up to a beachside bar—the server eyes us wary, asking for IDs—and I whip out my fake one smooth, calm as hell while Clay mirrors me—his scrutiny drags, decoding it like a secret scroll, but he finally shrugs and fetches our drinks. Two girls at the next table dive into Spanish chatter—they glance my way, one dropping—"Él es tan guapo"—and my Spanish game's tight, so I flip my hair, lean over—"Ustedes también son muy hermosas"—smooth as fuck, right? They burst into giggles—I shoot a cheeky grin, flag the server for tequila shots—eyes locked on the pair, twinning in shorts and crop tops, long brown hair flowing like they're synced to some unseen rhythm. One points at her friend—piggy nose, flirty lashes—"She's got a crush on you"—and I wink—"Swing over, sit on my lap"—next thing, Pig Face is on me, tasting of vodka, Red Bull, and trouble, while her doppelgänger locks lips with Clay, their fiery make-out blazing beside us.

"Pool party?" Pig Face purrs—we bounce from the bar, trailing their giggles down a side street to a mansion where the beats hit like a sledgehammer—the wraparound balcony pulses with bass so thick it shakes the ground beneath my boots, the walls towering up like a fortress scraping the sky as the door swings wide and chaos swallows us whole. Inside, bikini-clad girls sway under flashing lights—hips rolling, skin glistening with sweat and chlorine—while over at the gazebo, a pack of dudes clusters around a beer keg, their shouts rising over the clanking cups and cans that litter the grass like party shrapnel. The pool glitters wild—colorful beams dance across the water where inflatable flamingos bob to the rhythm, discarded cups and bottles floating like scars of the night—and I weave through the masses, the air thick with sunscreen, fried food, and that sweet, skunky waft of weed curling everywhere.

Pig Face drags us to Martin—the host—his bright orange Gators tee screaming loud, Ray-Bans perched on slick black hair that gleams under the lights, his veneers flashing wide in a grin that's all predator as he nods chill—"Hey, boys"—but my eyes snag on his girl beside him, sun-kissed blonde hair flowing over shoulders that frame a red bikini hugging her toned curves tight—her lips plump wild, a tease that hooks me hard when she smiles, and I wink back, slow and dark, feeling her gaze linger as I snag a six-pack from the cooler, brushing her arm deliberate and electric. She's a fucking vision—legs long and bronze, hips swaying like a dare—and I'm half-lost in her heat when Pig Face tugs me back, her voice droning about college plans for fall—some school I don't give a shit about—until the dream girl herself comes striding poolside, cigarette unlit, her scent of tequila, lemon, and reckless decisions cutting through as she leans in close—"You got a light?"—her hand resting on my thigh, honey dripping from her voice while I spark it, grazing her skin, her grin—"I'm Staci"—drawing me in—"Ethan"—and she spins away, hips curving a promise I'll chase.

Tequila shots slam with Clay and the girls—I ditch them fast, cutting through the kitchen's sea of bottles and shot-chugging dudes, the living room's soft glow fading as I climb the stairs—waiting by the bathroom, leaning against the wall when Staci materializes, eyes glinting with a spark that knows what's coming. The door swings open—we trade glances, sly and sharp—and I usher her inside, the lock clicking tight as her tongue dives down my throat, her hands frantic, pawing at my shirt while I grip her waist, pulling her hard against me—tequila and trouble flood my mouth, her bikini top slipping as I yank it aside, her gasps hot against my neck. Martin bangs the door—"Staci!"—his voice muffled through the wood—and I chug his beer, shoving my tongue deeper into her mouth, tasting her moan as we claw at each other—beats pound outside, bodies press the walls, and her nails dig into my back, the chaos ours 'til he bangs again, louder, but I'm lost in her fire, king of this fucked-up night.

Back by the pool, Staci's still on me—wasted, her red bikini pressed tight as tequila burns my throat—when Martin storms over, his orange Gators tee glaring under the pool lights, veneers flashing fury as he yanks my shirt hard and swings a fist at my face. The punch grazes my jaw—numb from shots, I barely flinch—but rage kicks wild, and I swing back, jabbing his gut with a sharp hook that doubles him over— Staci flies off my knee, sprawling on the grass with a yelp, his grunt's lost in the thumping bass as I head-butt him square, nose crunching under my skull, blood spraying hot and wet across my Nikes, painting them red in the flickering glow. He staggers—pathetic—and I keep kicking, boots slamming his ribs, his groans mixing with splashing water and shrieks——Staci's scream fuels me darker, wilder, and I land another blow, imagining the pipe from Jayden's, wishing I'd stabbed him deep, watched him bleed out over her screaming curves.

Clay grabs me hard—"E, let's go!"—his hands clamp my shoulders, hauling me back as Martin's buddies lurch forward, eyes glinting menace—but we're gone, bolting through the crowd—bodies part, cups crunch underfoot, the mansion's chaos fading as we sprint down the side street, adrenaline pumping fierce through my veins. Laughter rips from us—raw, untamed—echoing off the quiet houses as we weave past parked cars, the sea air slapping my face with salt and freedom—my split lip stings, blood smears my shirt, Nikes glisten red—and I yell—"Should've stabbed that fucker, Clay—let him bleed on her!"—the wild rush surging as Clay laughs harder, his vape glowing in the dark—"You're insane, bro!"—and we don't stop, running

blocks 'til the party's a distant hum, our breath ragged, hearts pounding like war drums.

We slow by a tucked-away beach—Clay snags a six-pack with our
fake IDs—and we crack cans against the Merc's hood, waves crashing
rhythmic as the buzz settles, my blood-stained kicks propped on the
bumper while the coastline stretches endless before us. Clay's grin
fades—he takes a swig, voice cutting through—"Dude, you ever feel
guilty about Willa with girls like Staci?"—and I gulp my beer, the cold
bite sharp as I shrug—"Nah, should I?"—my eyes on the surf, her
witchy pull tugging somewhere deep. "You're in love with her, right?"
he presses, and I lean back—"Guess so—love's weird—she's there,
always"—but his words linger, heavy—"Willa's awesome"—and I nod
slow—"Yeah, she is"—the night's chaos swirling with her hex, my wild
edge unbowed.

I lean against the Merc's hood, the metal warm under my palms as
the afternoon sun beats down. Clay cracks another beer, the six-pack's
empty cans glinting in the daylight while my blood-stained Nikes tap
restless, the fight's adrenaline still pumping raw through my veins.

"Unleash this fucker on the highway," I growl, voice scraped rough,
low as sin. Clay's grin splits wide—sharp, wild, mirroring mine—and
we dive into the Merc's leather guts, me riding shotgun, him gripping
the wheel like it's prey. The engine snarls alive, a deep, pissed-off
rumble shaking my boots as he peels us out, tires clawing asphalt with
a starving screech. I snag the last two beers—ice-cold, dripping like
blood—and shove one at Clay, Lil Pump's beats slamming through
the speakers, loud enough to crack skulls.

We hit the highway, and Clay stomps the gas like he's out for murder. The Merc roars—pure beast—slamming me back into the seat, power vibrating through my bones like a war drum. Wind rips through the open windows, tearing at my hair, stinging my split lip where Martin's blood's dried into a crusty smear on my shirt. I sip slow, beer biting sharp down my throat as palm trees blur into green smears—fuck this, I can't cage it—I let out a raw, unhinged howl, pure fucking thrill tearing outta me.

This is freedom, bitches.

This is king shit.

We slip off the highway, hauling ass to snag Douchebag Dad from the city. Then some dumb fuck darts across a side road—too fast, too late. Clay's tequila-and-beer-soaked reflexes are sludge, and we're a crash waiting to bleed. He slams the brakes—tires scream, a high-pitched death wail—as the Merc skids hard, fishtailing wild. My beer splashes cold across my crotch, and we smash into a brick wall with a thud that rattles my teeth. We barely jolt, but that wall's fucked—crumbles like a bitch under the hit.

Our eyes lock—silence cuts deep, thick with burnt rubber and the stink of our own panic. We shove the doors open, stepping out to face the carnage. The front grill's a mangled corpse—metal slashed open, left headlight dangling like a gouged eye, right fender gashed deep with claw-mark scars. Clay drags his fingers over a hood dent, tracing scratches carved into the silver like battle wounds. I glare at those busted headlights—jagged, grinning like a psycho's teeth.

It's fucking beautiful.

Clay's boots scuffing gravel as the afternoon sun glints off the wrecked grill—his breath's ragged, sharp, cutting through the quiet side road—and he starts pacing, hands raking his hair, vape trembling between his fingers as he puffs hard, smoke curling thick into the still air. "Dude, my dad's gonna kill me," he mutters—voice cracking low, frantic—"I'm so screwed, man—he'll take the truck, ground me for life—fuck, fuck, fuck!"—and he spins, smacking his palm against the hood, the dented metal groaning under his hit while his eyes dart wild, wide with panic, scanning the wreckage like it's a death sentence staring back. The beer's still buzzing in him—tequila too—I see it in the way he stumbles, the flush creeping up his neck—and he kicks the tire, muttering—"Insurance won't touch this—over the limit—cops'll nail me with a DUI—shit, E, what do I do?"

I lean back against the driver's door—beer can cold in my grip, the fight's blood drying stiff on my Nikes—and watch him unravel, his freakout spilling out raw and jagged, a mess I've never seen in him before—Clayboy, my bro, always steady, now cracking like the wall we hit. Something twists in my gut—sharp, unfamiliar—sympathy, maybe, sneaking up slow as I sip the last of my beer, the buzz softening my edges while his panic hardens his—his pacing's relentless, boots grinding dirt, vape puffing fast—and I feel it, this pull to fix it, not just for me but for him, the kid who's had my back since we were scrapping on skate ramps. "Fuck," I mutter—half to him, half to the wreck—and crush the can, tossing it aside as the idea glows clear—David's shop, my rap, no cops.

"Clay, chill—hold up," I say—voice steady, rough—stepping forward to grab his shoulders, stopping his frantic loop as his wild eyes lock mine, vape smoke curling between us—and I grin slow, dark—"I'll take it—tell your dad I drove, fucked it up—David'll fix it at the shop—no license, no cops hassling us." He stares—breath hitching—"Bro, you serious?"—and I nod, firm—"Yeah—swerved, hit the wall—my mess—I'll pay, split it with you—David'll be pissed, but better than you catching a DUI." His vape trembles—he puffs hard—"Dave'll shred you, man"—and I shrug—"Let him try—fucker's day's already shit—rather me than you in cuffs." Clay's grin flickers—small, shaky—"Damn, E—you're really doing this?"—and I slap his shoulder—"Bros for life, right? Fist pump seals it—deal's set—we're rolling."

Clay's vape puffs slow—his panic ebbs as my grin locks the plan, the wrecked Merc hulking beside us on this quiet side road—and I nudge him hard, voice low and steady—"Let's fetch your dad—beast's still rolling—time to face the fire." He nods—sharp, tense—and slides back into the driver's seat, the engine coughing alive with a ragged growl that hums through the leather as I swing in shotgun, the six-pack's empty cans rattling soft in the back—afternoon fades, the sun sinking low, painting the sky a bruised orange that bleeds into dusk as we pull out, tires scraping gravel, the wrecked grill glinting jagged under the last light. Clay's hands grip tight—knuckles pale—his vape tucked away—and I lean back, blood crusting my Nikes, split lip stinging sharp as the wind rushes through the open windows, tugging my hair wild while the road twists toward the city.

The Merc limps, metal groaning soft with every turn, the fender scraping like a wounded beast as we weave through thinning traffic, strip malls glowing faint against the dusk. Clay's quiet—his breath shallow, eyes darting to the dents slashing the hood—and I feel the wreck's weight settle heavier, my buzz fading into a gritty calm as the city looms closer, neon signs smearing red and blue streaks across the windshield. We roll up to the curb where Douchebag Dad waits—his leopard-print shirt catching the last sun's glare, gold cross swinging heavy as he paces—Clay double-parks, the bumper kissing concrete with a scrape—and we freeze, pulses kicking, waiting for the storm to break.

Dad's eyes slam into the Merc—his face twists, rage igniting red as dusk bleeds into night. He storms over, fists balled tight, voice exploding—"What the fuck?!"—his glare rakes the wreckage, wild and wide, the dented grill flashing under streetlights, headlight swinging like a gouged socket. He yanks the driver's door open—slams it shut with a bone-jarring bang—and fires the engine, tires shrieking as he peels us out, the fender clawing asphalt with a low, guttural scream. "This car fucking stinks of beer—and you two shits!"—his roar cuts the air, thick with venom as he swerves hard around a corner, the city blurring into a dark smear, shadows swallowing us whole.

He screeches to a stop—bolts out—slams both hands on the hood, the thud echoing as his frustration boils over. He spins on Clay, yanking him out by the collar—"What the fuck happened?!"—his voice a thunderclap, eyes blazing like he's ready to torch us both. Clay stumbles, cap slipping, but I'm already out—boots smack pavement—"I fucked it up," I say, voice rough, steady, cutting through his storm. "Talked Clay into letting me drive—no license, my bad—swerved, smashed the wall. David'll fix it. I'll bleed cash for it."

Dad's glare snaps to me, face purpling, veins popping—"Sixteen, you dumb fuck—no license—why the hell're you behind my wheel?!"—his mouth twitches, fury steaming off him like smoke. He pivots fast—fist flies—cracks my lip wide open, blood gushing hot down my chin, metallic sting flooding my tongue. "Fuck," I mutter, swiping it with my knuckles, grinning through the sting. He bellows—"Get in, both of you!"—and we scramble back, night pressing thick, his rage a live wire sparking as he guns it, bumper dragging, my blood dripping steady onto the leather.

The Merc rumbles low—night cloaks us thick as Douchebag Dad drives in silence, his knuckles white on the wheel, rage simmering quiet now, a storm held tight—Clay slumps beside me, his breath shallow, eyes darting to the wrecked fender scraping asphalt with every turn, the sound a jagged whine cutting the stillness. My split lip throbs—blood crusts my chin, drips slow onto my shirt—and I sit shotgun, boots braced against the floor, the wrecked beast's groan filling the void where words should be—Dad's glare burns ahead, streetlights streaking gold across his leopard-print shirt, the gold cross glinting faint as we roll through the city's edge, shadows swallowing the road. Tension chokes the air—Clay's vape stays tucked, my buzz fades to a dull ache—and we ride wordless, the engine's hum a lifeline, pulling us steady toward home where the real shit waits.

We pull into the driveway—gravel crunches under tires, the bumper kissing concrete with a scrape—and Dad's out fast, marching to the door, ringing the bell like a madman, his fist pounding relentless 'til David swings it open, shirt rumpled, eyes squinting into the dusk-turned-night. Dad's voice cuts sharp—"Get out here, Dave—look at this fucking mess"—and he jabs a finger at the Merc, its wrecked grill glinting under the porch light as David steps out, barefoot, his jaw tightening slow while Dad's arms flail, shouting curses—"Your kid fucked my car!"—and I ease out, Clay trailing, my boots hitting the ground heavy, blood still smeared fresh from Dad's punch. David's gaze lands on me—narrows at my lip, the split red and raw, then flicks to the stains crusting my Nikes—and his eyes harden, sharp as blades—"What happened to your lip, Ethan?"

I stay quiet, blood still trickling from my lip, grinning dark as Douchebag Dad snarls at David, "I clocked him—fucking trashed my Merc!" David's face twists, rage erupting fast—"You hit my kid, Chad, you piece of shit?!"—and his fist rockets out, smashing Chad's jaw with a wet crack that rips across the lawn. Chad staggers, but David's on him—locks him in a headlock, pounding down hard, knuckles splitting skin as they crash into the grass like rabid bears. Chad's leopard shirt shreds wide, gold cross swinging crazy as he flails back—fists slice air, missing wild—grunts tearing outta him, raw and loud into the thickening night.

They roll, tearing up the pristine turf—David's sweat gleams under the porch light, Chad's slick skin catching dusk's last glow as fists fly feral—Chad grazes David's cheek, barely stirring the air, and they slam into a flowerbed, dirt exploding in clumps. "My fucking car!" Chad roars, voice a guttural howl, but David's bellow—"He's my kid, asshole!"—cuts deeper, their thrashing a messy blur of rage and ripped fabric. Clay and I stand rooted, my grin widening—fuck, it's beautiful—neighbors creep out now, a loose ring of wide-eyed vultures, their whispers buzzing like flies over the thuds and snarls splitting the quiet street, shadows stretching long across this middle-class cage.

Mom bursts from the house—her face twists tight with fear, Kacey clutched close to her chest—and her voice bellows across the neighborhood, sharp and desperate—"STOP! Stop right now!"—but they don't hear, don't care—David's fist cracks Chad's jaw, Chad's elbow slams back, missing by a hair, stirring a gust that rustles Mom's hair as she dives between them, hands shoving at David's chest like she can tame the beast roaring inside him. "Get off him!" she screams—her voice splits the air—and Chad lunges, fist swinging wild, grazing David's shoulder as they stumble apart, panting heavy—Mom spins to us—"Get inside now!"—her glare cutting through, arms folded tight, but Clay and I drift to the living room window, peering out with the neighbors, watching the chaos unfurl like a fucked-up show.

Chad staggers up—points at the Merc's wreckage, his hands flailing everywhere—"Look at this shit!"—his voice raw, ragged—and David's face flushes crimson, fists clenching as he steps forward—Mom clutches his chest, holding him back—"Enough, Dave!"—her voice cracks, pleading now—Chad's still shouting—"Fucking totaled!"—and David's growling—"He's sixteen, Chad!"—their yells tangle, loud and messy—then simmer, words softening slow as they circle the car, Chad tracing dents, David nodding stiff—Mom's grip eases—they talk, low and tense—hands shake, grudging—and the neighbors peel back, doors clicking shut as the street quiets, night falling thick and heavy.

Chad spins—"Clayton, let's go!"—his voice cuts sharp, final—and Clay pats my shoulder hard, a solid thump—"Thanks, bro—I owe you big time"—his grin flickers, quick and shaky, before he jogs to the Merc, its front bumper scraping the road loud as they peel out, the wrecked beast limping off into the dark. I lock eyes with David through the window—he's storming back, night shadowing his rage—and the front door looms ahead, my split lip throbbing, blood crusting my shirt, ready for the next storm to break.

The front door bursts open—David charges in like a bull, night spilling behind him as his rage ignites the room—his arm sweeps wild across the entrance hall table, papers fluttering frantic, a vase of flowers shattering sharp against the hardwood with a crash that echoes through the house. "Do you think I'm made of money?"—his bellow shakes the walls, thick legs waddling fast as he storms toward me, eyes blazing fire—and I stand rooted by the window, split lip throbbing, blood crusting my shirt, Nikes stained red from Martin's nose while the air turns thick, electric with his fury. He snatches Mom's Shiva head ornament from the side shelf—lifts it high, veins bulging in his neck—and smashes it down hard, the stone cracking into shards, a broken eye glinting up at me from the floor as his roar fills the space—"I'll fix that idiot's car for free, but is it free? I'm paying for your crap again!"

Chaos erupts—his hands grab a coffee cup from the table, hurling it fast at my head—I duck, breath catching as it slams the wall, splattering dark across my shirt—then a coffee-table book flies, thick and heavy, followed by another, the third smacking square into my face, a dull thud ringing my skull as I stagger back, blood trickling fresh from my lip. He's on me—massive paws clamp my neck, lifting me off the ground—my boots kick air—and he slams me against the wall, cement biting hard into my spine, pain shooting raw through my bones while Mom stands back, arms folded tight, her glare cold as stone, not moving an inch to stop him. "What the fuck were you thinking, you useless piece of shit?"—his voice thunders, rings on his fingers cutting scratches into my skin as he slaps my head hard—"Motherfucking waste of space!"—another slap stings—"Are you even listening?"—his bellow grows louder—"Do you have any brains in that thick skull?"—slap after slap rains down—"I'm spending my cash fixing your mess!"

My ears ring—a thousand bells clanging wild—his hands drop, rough and sudden, and he spins away, shaking his head as he sur-

veys the wreckage—shattered Shiva, scattered papers, coffee pooling dark—his growl low—"Clean this mess up"—before stalking off,
footsteps thudding heavy up the stairs. Mom's glare lingers—silent,
cutting—then she turns, following him without a word, leaving me
slumped against the wall, breath ragged, body aching sharp—Brent
slips in, brush and dustpan in hand—"You okay?"—his voice soft
as he scoops shards, pointing—"Your head's bleeding." I touch
my forehead—wince at the sting—"What'd that fucker throw, the
Bible?"—we chuckle low, grim, and I help sweep, the mess a mirror
to the chaos inside me.

Night deepens—midnight pings my phone—Clay's name glows—I
check the back door, find a white envelope wedged tight—Oxy tabs
spill from his ER stash, a crumpled note—"I owe you big time,
bro"—and I pocket it, my bruised face grinning faint in the dark.

VAPES AND VICTIMS

The beach sprawls wide under a late afternoon sun—waves snarl low, crashing steady as I stalk the wet sand, blood-crusted Nikes sinking into the tide-packed edge, leaving faint, gritty prints. Willa's beside me, black boots stomping like she's ready to hex the shore, red hair lashing wild in the salty wind, denim skirt flapping, bikini top flashing a dare beneath. Spring break's noise fades behind us—nobody out here but us—and I drop hard onto the dry dunes up the slope, sprawling back as hot sand claws my bruised skin. David's fists still throb in my ribs, my neck, my split lip raw and pulsing. Willa flops close—her knee jams mine, a jolt sparking through me—her eyes lock on my marks, narrowing sharp as she leans in, witchy hum coiling tight like a noose I'd wear proud.

Her fingers trace a bruise—David's purple bloom stamped on my arm—cool against my heat, slow and deliberate, and I grin, letting her stir that dark flicker I crave. "Fuck, E—what'd that prick do?"—her voice cuts rough, low, just for me—and I tilt my head, sand grinding into my hair—"Clay smashed Douchebag Dad's Merc—I owned it—David flipped, fists flying like always." Her gaze hits my lip—blood's cracked, flaking—and her thumb brushes it, lingering, eyes glinting hex-dark—"He's a bastard—always been." I laugh, low and mean—"Yeah, but I'd gut 'em all—Chad, David, any fucker who swings—feel that rush, blood hot on my hands." Her breath hitches—fingers freeze—then her smirk curls, wicked—"You've been itching for that since we were kids—slashing deep, watching 'em bleed."

I shove up on my elbows—sand sticks to my shirt, bruises kicking as the sun bleeds gold into the waves—and she's right, fuck, she's always been right. Willa's seen it since forever—that itch I bury, flaring hot when I cracked Martin's nose, gripped that pipe at Jayden's—her freaky Monster High dolls glaring from her shelf while Kayla's prissy American Girl shit sat soft. Two fires, and Willa's hex always burned me first. "Fuck yeah," I growl, voice scraped—"I'd carve 'em slow—David's throat, Chad's guts, even Rick if he sniffed Kayla—feel the blade sing." She leans in—red hair grazes my cheek, sage and sea choking me alive—"You'd be free, E—fucking alive"—her grin's a blade, sharp as the tide sucking out, tying me to that edge I'd kill for, seeds of chaos sprouting wild in the dusk.

Waves growl low as we peel off the dunes—sun's dipping, painting the Civic's faded shell gold in the lot. I kick sand off my Nikes—blood's faint, crusted from David's beatdown—and Willa's boots scuff beside me, phone in hand, voice slicing the breeze—"Clay and Kayla's at the mall—let's roll." I snatch my board, ribs screaming sharp, and nod—she's already striding, hair whipping like a storm as we pile into the car. Keys jangle from her finger—engine coughs, then hums steady, vibrating through my soles as she guns it, road stretching out like a vein begging to bleed.

We ride smooth—afternoon light spills through the windshield, casting long shadows over the dashboard as palm trees sway lazy along the streets, their fronds blurring into streaks of green while strip malls and gas stations slide past, baking under the sun's last glare. Willa's hands grip the wheel—her denim skirt rides up as she shifts gears—and my split lip stings with every jolt, the bruises pulsing under my shirt as I lean back, watching the city creep closer, the mall's sprawl looming just beyond the next turn. She doesn't speak—her witchy edge simmers quiet—and I let the silence sit, the car's growl filling the space until we roll into the parking lot—tires crunch asphalt, easing to a stop near the food court entrance—and I step out, board tucked under my arm, the air thick with mall buzz as we head inside.

Fluorescent lights glare off tiled floors—kids weave through crowds, their chatter bouncing loud as I spot Clay by the food court, his cap twisted back, leaning against a table where Kayla's flipping her blonde ponytail, her skirt swishing as she laughs too easy with him, her voice bright and sharp cutting through the din. I saunter over—Willa's boots click beside me, her presence a shadow—and call out, "Yo, Clayboy," my voice rough with a tease as he turns, smirking wide—"E, 'bout time"—and I lean in close, eyes flicking to Kayla—"You into Kayla or what?"—the words slip out light, testing him as she spins toward me, her curves catching the light—tight top hugging her chest, hips swaying smooth—and Clay laughs—"Nah, bro—just chilling"—but his grin flickers, quick and unsteady, a hint I catch before it's gone.

Willa's eyes narrow—she catches my tease, her witchy hum sharpening as she steps forward, her voice slicing low—"What's that about Kayla?"—and I barely turn before she's on it—her gaze locks onto Kayla, who's mid-laugh, clueless 'til Willa's words hit hard—"You think you're slick, cheer bitch?"—venom drips thick as she closes the gap fast—Kayla whirls back—"What's your deal, Willa?"—and it ignites—Willa's hand shoots out, snagging Kayla's ponytail, yanking fierce—blonde strands tangle tight in her fist—Kayla shrieks—"Get off me!"—and swings wild, nails clawing at Willa's arm—hair-pulling turns feral, their yells rising over the food court clamor as Clay jumps in—"Whoa, chill!"—but I hang back, grinning dark, the triangle flaring hot—jealousy's a spark catching fire.

Kayla shoves hard—Willa stumbles, boots skidding on tile—her red hair flies as she lunges again, fingers snagging Kayla's top, ripping a seam with a sharp tear—Kayla's "You psycho!"—rings loud—and Willa snaps back—"Stay away from him!"—her glare flicks to me, then Clay—possession burning fierce in her eyes—mall kids gawk, phones out, filming the mess as Clay grabs Willa's arm—"Enough!"—and I step in, voice rough—"Let it go, witch"—pulling her back, her chest heaving fast, eyes blazing—Kayla brushes her skirt, glaring sharp—"Fucking crazy"—and I laugh low—"Fuck yeah"—bruises pulsing steady, the heat of their clash sinking deep, my edge cutting sharper as night creeps close outside.

***

Willa's witchy snap still echoes—her "Stay away from him" ringing sharp as I kick my board down the street. I text Clay—"Ryan's party?"—his "Hell yeah, bro" pings back fast—and Willa's call buzzes—her voice low, demanding—"Where you at, E?"—but I grin, rough—"Out—later, witch"—and cut her off, ditching her pull, my boots hitting pavement as I roll toward Ryan's place, night's heat curling thick, promising chaos I can taste. The bruises ache—David's marks blooming dark—and I crave the rush.

Ryan's crib pulses—beats thump heavy through open windows, spilling out onto the lawn where kids cluster, red cups glinting under string lights strung crooked across the porch—vape haze drifts lazy, weed and cheap beer stinking sweet as I step inside, the air thick with sweat and laughter. Ryan—some jock from school—nods me in—"E, my man"—his grin loose, buzzed—and I weave through the crowd—bodies sway tight, music shaking the walls—until I spot Kayla on a sagging couch, her skirt riding high, tight pink panties underneath cutting sharp above her thighs, top clinging to her curves as she flips her blonde ponytail, vape in hand. She sees me—eyes glint—and pats the spot beside her—"Hey, E, sit"—her voice purrs hot, pulling me down as her thigh presses mine, heat sparking through denim—fuck, she's a flame I can't dodge.

She's all over me—her fingers tease my arm, tracing David's bruises slow and deliberate—her vape puffs cherry clouds that swirl thick around us, sweet on her breath as she leans close—"No Willa tonight?"—and I smirk—"Ditched her—free man"—my voice rough, bruises throbbing under her touch as she shifts, shorts riding higher—her heat's a dare, her laugh ringing soft—"Good choice"—and she presses tighter, her chest brushing my side, vape haze wrapping us close while she teases—"Look at you—wild boy—all beat up"—her fingers graze my split lip, lingering hot—my pulse kicks hard, lust flaring dark as she grins—"Hot with bruises, E." I laugh low—"Fuck yeah"—and she's giggling, cherry vape puffing soft against my neck—"Walk me home?"—her dare hangs heavy—and I nod—"Let's roll"—leading her out, the party's thump fading as we hit the street.

Night cloaks us—stars glint faint above quiet houses—her hips sway beside me, shorts cutting tight, vape glowing as we wander blocks, her laugh spilling sharp into the stillness—bruises ache with every step, fueling me wilder. She stops—leans against a fence—"You're so hot like this, E—beat up, badass"—her voice drips low, eyes blazing—then she's on me, lips crashing hard, cherry tang flooding my mouth—I grip her waist, pulling her fierce—shorts dig into my palms, her heat searing through—fuck, it's primal—I bite her lip sharp, tasting blood faint and sweet—she gasps, nails clawing my neck, her moan vibrating hot—my tongue claims hers, vape haze swirling thick as I press her against the fence, stakes climbing wild—Willa's hex a ghost—Kayla's fire mine—my edge cuts deeper, night swallowing us whole.

I roll home—bruises aching, lip stinging—shower steam fills the bathroom as her DMs hit my phone before I'm even dry—"U feel bad about what happened?"—her words glow—I grin, typing—"Nah, u?"—her reply's quick—"A lil. U r my BFF's bf, kinda weird"—and I tease—" Did u like the kiss?"—"it was gr8 kiss"—she fires back—my grin curls—"Then let's do it again sometime. Lol. Our secret Kayz. Just between us"—her text pings—"U promise never to tell Willa?"—"I swear. Scouts honor"—I shoot—and she's on—"Were u ever a scout?"—"Nah but that doesn't matter lol"—her "lol okay" seals it—water beats down—I jerk myself off in the shower, imagining pushing her into the woods, stabbing 'til her blood runs out, soaking the earth below—dark, wild, alive—my edge cuts free.

Tarot & Hexes

Morning light claws through my blinds, stabbing me awake—sheets choke my legs, twisted tight, Kayla's cherry bite still burning my lips from last night's feral sink, her blood's ghost tang spiking through the dull throb of David's fists etched deep in my bruises. My split lip's stiff, crusted under my thumb as I roll outta bed, yanking on yesterday's jeans with a rough tug—Willa's witchy hum claws at my skull, her mall snarl—"Stay away from him"—ringing low, but I shove it down, snatching my board from the corner, wood cold and solid in my grip. I jam my Nikes on, laces biting tight—Chad's fucked-up Merc's gone, David's storm a dead echo—and I'm out, air hitting crisp as I kick off hard toward Willa's, wheels grinding pavement, sun clawing higher, shadows stretching long and mean across the street.

Willa's house rises ahead—an old relic, peeling paint flaking off clapboard walls, dark windows staring blank in the new build sprawl—I roll up, porch steps creaking under my boots with every slow climb—Palo Santo drifts thick through the cracked front door, sage curling faint in the air as I push inside, my footsteps echoing soft on the warped wooden stairs leading up to her room. The air shifts heavy when I step through her doorway—mugwort and candle wax fill my lungs, and I see her sprawled across her bed, black sheets tangled around her bare legs, her red hair spilling wild over the pillows like a river of fire catching the morning light. Tarot cards lie spread out before her on the mattress—she's staring at the Death card, its skeletal grin looming sharp under the flicker of a red candle on her altar—and she's painting, her fingers dipping into a pot of red paint, smearing wet runes across a canvas propped against her knees, the crimson dripping slow onto the sheets as she mutters low under her breath—"Evil's in him—Kayla's next"—her voice weaving a spell that hums through the room.

I drop my board against the wall—thuds soft, a quiet kill—and Willa's eyes snap up, glinting like broken glass, raking over the purple bruises snaking under my shirt, my split lip crusted red from David's fists. She shifts on the bed, black lace top riding up, tossing the canvas aside—crimson runes smear her fingers, wet and bloody. "You're back—marked uglier," she says, voice slicing low through the sage-choked air. She leans in, tracing a bruise on my arm—cool, deliberate, her painted touch sparking my heat—and I smirk, letting her linger as I drop onto the bed's edge, mattress groaning under me. "Chad's Merc's a corpse—fists flew," I growl, rough and steady. She nods slow—"Evil's in you—always was—Kayla's next"—her grip clamps my wrist, runes glistening on the canvas as she drags the Death card close, its scythe licking the candle's flame.

She paints another rune—red streaks drip across the canvas, staining her sheets as she leans closer—her breath brushes my neck, sage and wax thick in the air—and she says, "I see it growing—darkness owns you—she's too close"—her voice hums dark, steady as she traces the card's edge with a crimson finger, her eyes glinting wild. "Fuck yeah," I say—my voice cuts rough—"I feel it—David's blood, Chad's—I'd kill 'em all, taste that rush"—and her gaze snaps sharp, fury flaring sudden as she pulls back—"I see how you look at her—Kayla—those eyes you give each other"—her voice rises, raw and jagged—"If I catch you fucking her, I'll kill you both—rip her throat, gut you slow"—her painted hand slams the canvas, red splashing wild as she shoves the Death card at me—her witchy hum turns hex, her eyes blazing—"Get out—go!"—and she kicks at me, her boot slamming my thigh.

I stagger up—board in hand—her fury pulses hot as I back toward the door—"Fuck, Willa"—my grin curls dark, bruises throbbing—and she yells—"Out!"—her voice a spell cracking the air, runes dripping red as I hit the stairs, boots thudding fast down warped wood—Palo Santo chokes thick behind me, her hex ringing in my ears as I burst out.

Willa's "I'll kill you both" echoes raw in my skull as I storm out her creaky witch house—the noon sun glares sharp off peeling paint, sage smoke trailing me down the porch steps, my boots slamming gravel with every pissed-off stride. Her red runes flash—her boot's kick stings my thigh—and my bruises pulse hot from David's fists, my split lip cracking fresh as I snatch my skateboard, kicking off hard down the street—wind whips my hair wild, the quiet pavement blurring under my Nikes while fury burns low in my gut, Willa's hex a live wire I can't shake—she's flipped, evil as fuck, and I'm done with her shit today. I weave past houses waking slow—sun climbing higher, shadows shrinking—and aim for Clayton's place, my pulse hammering fast, needing something raw to burn this off.

Clay's house sits squat under the beating sun—his truck hulks in the drive, faded paint glinting as I roll up, kicking my board to a stop—my boots hit the cracked walkway, and I bang the door loud—Clay swings it open, cap twisted back—"E, what's up, bro?"—his grin flickers easy, but I shove past—"Willa's lost it—fucking psycho"—my voice cuts rough, fists clenching as I drop onto his couch, the springs groaning under me. He grabs beers from the fridge—tosses me one, cold and slick—and I crack it open, swigging hard, the bite sharp against my lip as I pull my phone, texting Kayla—"Come over—Clay's"—my grin curls dark, bruises throbbing—Clay flops beside me—"She kick you out?"—and I nod—"Threatened to kill me—Kayla too—fucking hex shit"—his laugh spills—"She's wild, man"—but I'm already buzzing, waiting for her spark.

Kayla's here fast—her denim shorts hug her thighs, crop top tight on her curves—she flips her blonde ponytail, eyes glinting sharp—"Hey, E"—her voice purrs low, and Clay smirks—"Hey, Kay"—but she's on me, sliding onto the couch beside me—her thigh brushes warm against mine, nails grazing my arm where David's marks bloom purple—and I grin—"Hey, trouble"—my voice rough as she leans close—"Willa pissed?"—her tease lands soft—and I laugh—"Fucking flipped—kicked me out"—her giggle spills—"Good"—and she shifts, her scent—cherry and sweat—hitting me hard—Clay's still here, sipping his beer—"You two are chaos"—but I don't care—my hand finds her waist—"Come here"—and I pull her toward his room, the door clicking shut behind us.

We hit his bed—sheets twist fast as she climbs over me, her nails digging into my shoulders—hot, quick—her shorts ride up, thighs pressing tight as she straddles me—I yank her down under the covers, my hands gripping hard—her cheer top lifts, skin warm against my bruises—and she's kissing me, cherry tang flooding my mouth—fuck, it's primal—I bite her lip sharp, tasting blood faint and sweet—she gasps, nails clawing my neck—my tongue dives deep, her moan vibrating hot as I press her into the mattress, covers tangling wild—lust flares fast, no linger—her shorts scrape my palms, her heat searing through—Willa's hex burns distant—Kayla's fire takes me—my edge cuts raw, quick, night nowhere near as we finish, breath ragged, her nails still dug in.

Lockers & Drama

I roll into school late—morning sun beats down hard as my board grinds to a stop near the gym, bruises pulsing raw from David's fists, my split lip stinging fresh under the heat—and I spot Willa storming across the field, her red hair whipping wild like a flame cutting through the crowd, her black boots kicking dirt as she heads straight for cheer practice where Kayla's flipping her ponytail, skirt swishing short over tight shorts. Willa's pissed—her witchy hum burns dark after yesterday's hex rant—and I lean against the bleachers, watching her close in, my grin curling rough as the air thickens with her fury—Kayla's laugh rings out from the squad, oblivious 'til Willa's shadow falls over her, sharp and heavy.

Willa corners her fast—cheer girls scatter, their chatter fading as she grabs Kayla's arm, yanking her from a twirl—"You with him last night?"—her voice slices low, raw with jealousy, eyes blazing fire under the sun's glare—and Kayla pulls free, smirking sharp—"What's it to you, witch?"—her tone's a tease, blonde hair glinting as she steps back, hands on hips, her shorts hugging tight—fuck, she's baiting her.

Willa's fists clench—her painted nails dig into her palms, red from yesterday's runes—"I see how you look at him—Ethan's mine—were you with him?"—her words spit fast, venom dripping as her glare cuts deeper—Kayla's smirk widens—"Maybe—jealous much?"—and Willa's eyes blaze hotter, stepping close—"I'll kill you if you fucked him—rip that smirk off your face"—her voice turns hex, low and wild—Kayla laughs—"Try it"—and shoves her, Willa stumbling back, boots skidding dirt.

I watch—bruises throbbing—Willa's fury's a live wire, her witchy edge snapping as she lunges—Kayla dodges, her squad gasping—and Willa's hand swings, missing by a hair—"Stay away, cheer bitch"—her growl echoes sharp across the field—Kayla flips her off—"Fuck you, Willa"—and spins back to practice, leaving Willa seething, her chest heaving fast—jealousy peaks raw as she turns, spotting me—her glare cuts—"You're next"—and storms off, boots pounding turf—my grin stays, dark and steady, Kayla's heat still burning in my blood, Willa's hex a spark pre-murder.

Afternoon drags—school's hum fades as I skate out, sun dipping low, my phone buzzing hot in my pocket—I pull it, bruised knuckles flexing, and see Jayden's name glow—his text hits quick—"Yo, E—Kayla's mine, back off"—his cocky drawl drips through the words, funny as fuck. I laugh low—my split lip splits wider—picturing his buzzed head, that "cut here" tat on his neck, his lean frame swaying high at his crib—enemy or not, this shit's gold—my grin curls dark as I type—"Fuck off, J—she's free game"—and hit send, pocketing it fast, the buzz of rage seeding slow in my gut.

He fires back—phone pings again—"U think u tough, E? Watch ur-self"—and I snort—cocky prick's got no clue—Kayla's cherry kiss, her nails last night, flash hot—my Nikes grip the board as I kick harder down the street, wind tugging my hair—Jayden's text a spark, funny and quick, but his "mine" stings sharp—my edge cuts darker,—bruises pulse from David's fists, Willa's hex—"I'll kill you both"—mixing raw with Kayla's heat—Jayden's rage a late Build-Up flare I'll burn later—my "Fuck yeah" hums low, stakes climbing wild as dusk settles thick.

Swimming Pool & Eight Balls

Afternoon sun beats down hard—I skate up Kayla's street, board grinding asphalt under my Nikes, bruises pulsing raw from David's fists, my split lip itching fresh as Willa's hex—"I'll kill you both"—snaps sharp in my skull, Jayden's "Kayla's mine" buzzing faint like a fly I'd swat—her house looms ahead, blue and white balloons bobbing wild over the fence, silver streamers glinting sharp like cheer squad knives cutting through the haze—my boots hit gravel as I kick to a stop, the air thick with chlorine and grilled meat, kids' shrieks spilling loud from the backyard—Kayla's 17th pulsing alive, a storm I'm diving into headfirst—fuck yeah, I'm here—Willa's rage a ghost, Kayla's heat pulling me in.

I push through the front door—blue streamers twist overhead, white balloons bob against the ceiling, silver pom-poms shimmer on tables—Kayla's cheer squad's mark everywhere—and I weave inside, boots scuffing hardwood as family photos catch my eye—Kayla at five grins gap-toothed on the wall, blonde pigtails swinging, her mom beside her, smile tipped high in faded Polaroids—then Kayla at ten, braces gleaming, pool float under her arm—pictures line the hall, a timeline of her I drink in slow—my fingers graze a frame, her dad's grilling apron in the background—smoke wafts now, real and sharp, burgers sizzling out back where he stands, spatula flipping meat, kids splashing wild in the pool—blue water glints under sunlight, their yells cutting through the thumping pop beats spilling from speakers.

Her mom swans through—oversized shades perch on her nose, vodka OJ sloshing in one hand, poodle yapping shrill in the other—her blonde hair swings loose, shades glinting as she drifts past—pool water sparkles beyond glass doors, kids cannonballing loud—and I slip toward the stairs, boots quiet on carpet—her mom's voice floats up—"Are you lost, Ethan?"—her tone slurs soft, curious—and I grin back—"Nah, just exploring"—my voice rough, dodging her as I climb, her poodle's bark chasing me—vodka OJ tilts in her grip, shades hiding her stare—my bruises throb, lust curling dark as I hit the landing, Kayla's room calling me up.

Her door's ajar—pop music seeps out, bubblegum beats buzzing soft—and I shove in, air turning thick with her—pink walls glow under fairy lights, stuffed animals clutter shelves—bears, rabbits, a one-eyed dog sagging—cheer trophies shine gold, ribbons curling lazy, travel pics pinned sloppy—Kayla in Paris, Rome, sand dusting her toes—her teal bed's a fucked-up mess, sheets knotted wild. She slips in behind me, purple bikini clinging wet from the pool, dripping trails down her thighs—blonde ponytail swings heavy, water gleaming on her skin—fuck, she's a live wire. Her eyes flash—"Hey, E—birthday treat?"—and I kick the door shut—lock snaps hard—grinning rough—"Fuck yeah."

She slams into me—wet heat hits like a wave, bikini sticking tight as she yanks me to the bed—sheets snag fast. I pin her down, knees locking her hips, her wrists trapped under my grip—her nails claw my arms, raking hot lines over bruises—and I smirk, peeling bikini strings slow with one hand, the other pinning her harder. Her lips crash mine, sunshine and vodka OJ bursting sweet—I bite her neck, teeth sinking deep below her jaw, blood prickling faint under my tongue—she yelps sharp—"Ethan!"—her moan rips out, raw and loud. My tongue claims her, her nails gouging my back—sheets twist tighter—her thighs buck against mine, bikini top sliding loose—my shirt tears—lust cuts feral. Willa's hex hums faint, a ghost—Kayla's fire owns me now—downstairs fades, kids splashing, Dad's grill sizzling distant.

Willa's downstairs—pissed—her witchy hum seeps up through the floor—her boots stomp hard, her voice slicing sharp—"Where's Kayla?"—Clay's "Chill, Willa" fades as she snarls—"That bitch—he's with her!"—and I grin under Kayla's heat, her nails digging deeper—Willa's eyes blaze somewhere below—fury peaking wild—her "I'll kill them" from yesterday rings—Kayla's breath quickens—"More, E"—her whisper's hot—my edge cuts sharper—triangle stakes soar—Willa fumes blind, my darkness claiming Kayla here—party thumps on—night's shadow creeping close outside.

Kayla's birthday cake sits gutted on the table, blue frosting smeared across plates as dusk turns black, the pool glowing eerie under fairy lights—teens cluster tight around it, vodka sloshing in red cups, their laughs slurring loud over the water's slap—my Nikes pace the deck, bruises pulsing raw from David's fists, split lip stinging as I sip Mom's vodka OJ, the poodle yapping shrill at her heels while she sways shades slippling up to her bed leaving the kids alone. The air's thick—chlorine, sweat, booze—and I feel Willa's hex, her witchy hum simmering low after the bed rush with Kayla—fuck, her nails still burn in my head—when Jayden rolls in, boots stomping loud, his buzzed head glinting—tequila bottle swinging expensive in one hand, silver paper tied with a pink bow in the other—cocaine, wrapped like a gift—and my grin curls dark, edge cutting sharp as he struts to Kayla, her purple bikini dripping pool water under the lights.

Jayden's clingy as fuck—his hand lingers on Kayla's shoulder, fingers dragging slow over her wet skin, claiming her—her laugh spills too bright, too loose—and I picture my blade kissing his throat, slicing that "cut here" tat wide, blood gushing hot over my knuckles, his red eyes dimming. My pulse slams, lust and rage churning thick as he tears into the coke—silver paper rips, teens swarm, cups diving in—Kayla's "Jay, chill" gets lost. I slide in smooth, voice rough—"Sweet haul"—and snag the tequila bottle, glass cool in my grip. His glare burns—"Fuck off, E"—but I feint left, bump his arm hard—coke packet slips as he swings wild, fist cutting air. I snatch it mid-fall, silver bow crumpling in my fist, boots already dodging his sloppy lunge—he snarls—"She's mine, asshole"—and I grin dark—"Fuck yeah"—coke scorching my pocket, dark itch flaring—Kayla's skin still hums from his touch, mine screaming from hers.

Willa's storm brews—I feel her boots pounding up as I bolt, her "Where's Ethan?" slashing through the vodka fog—Jayden's "Upstairs, bitch" trails off. I grab her wrist—"We're out"—and we're gone, boards carving asphalt hard to my place—night chokes us, wheels growling, her red hair whipping wild, hex humming hot. My room's a black cave—door slams, lock clicks—we strip fast, bare under my sheets. Charli XCX's *Boom Clap* throbs jagged from the stereo, pulsing chaos as I cut lines—razor splits the coke fine on the nightstand, hands steady, bruises kicking alive. Willa's eyes sear—"You were in her room"—her voice bites low, sharp—coke hits my nose, electric jolt frying my veins—"Nothing went down"—I rasp, lying rough. She snorts a line, head snapping back—"My gut's screaming you're full of shit"—hex coils tight—my high spikes—"Fuck, Willa—always projecting your old scars?"

Her fury ignites—"Don't twist this—you're hers, I fucking see it"—nails gouge my arm, drawing blood—my shove's hard—"Bullshit, you're blind"—coke jagged in my chest—her glare burns—"Kayla's next, you prick—I'm not dumb"—sheets rip as she leaps up—"We're done—break's on"—boots slam the floor, her voice cracking wild—"You'll crawl back, but I'm out"—door flies open, hinges groan—she storms off, red hair a vanishing flame. Rage boils hot—fuck her—Charli's beat pounds, my hands tremble, coke dust sticking—Willa's hex fractures—phone glows—I text Kayla—"Run away with me"—grin twists dark, high roaring—bruises throb—Kayla's cherry bite, Willa's curse—triangle's a live wire—rage roots deep—night eats her steps—I'm alone, electric, ready to torch it all.

CURSES & DREAMS

Morning cracks hard—sun claws through blinds, Kayla's "Run away with me" text searing my skull, Willa's "Take a break" still raw from last night's coke-charged storm. Bruises throb deep from David's fists, split lip stinging as I roll outta bed, yanking jeans on fast—Willa's hex hums a ghost I kick aside, snagging my board. Nikes hit the floor—Chad's wrecked Merc's long gone, David's rage a dead echo—and I'm out, skating hard down streets frying under noon heat, wheels grinding, wind ripping my hair wild toward Kayla's place, her purple bikini flash burning my veins—fuck yeah, I'm hers—Willa's calls can choke.

Kayla's house looms quiet—blue balloons droop from last night's bash, silver streamers sag over the fence. I kick my board still, boots crunching gravel—my phone buzzes sharp, Willa's name flaring—ignored—vibrates again as I hit the porch, sage stink fading fast. Kayla swings the door wide—tight shorts grip her thighs, crop top riding high—blonde ponytail flips, eyes glinting—"Hey, E"—voice low, a spark. I step in—"Hey, Kayz"—rough, bruises pulsing—Willa's call buzzes once more, silenced cold. Kayla grins—"She raging?"—I smirk—"Fuck her"—my hand claims her waist, her heat jolting through—phone hums dead—Willa's hex a shadow—Kayla's fire owns me.

She pulls me in—living room's empty, pool glints blue beyond glass—grill's cold, Mom's vodka OJ ghosted—my boots scuff hardwood—Willa's calls pile up, frantic—I mute the bitch—Kayla's fingers graze mine—"Your pool?"—I nod sharp—"Fuck yeah"—and grab her wrist, tugging her out. Stairs skip, her bare feet slap floors—we're gone, my board carving asphalt hard, her laugh spilling bright as we blaze through quiet streets, noon sun torching the sprawl.

My place hits—driveway's cracked, empty—Chad's Merc a memory, David's storm a dull ache. I kick my board aside, gate creaking as we hit the backyard—pool shimmers blue, water still and sharp under the glare, lawn chairs crooked on patchy grass. I rip my shirt off—bruises bloom dark across my chest—Kayla sheds her shorts, purple bikini flashing as she dives, water exploding cold, flecking my jeans. I ditch boots, jeans hit the deck—cannonball in, waves slamming around me, soaking my skin. She surfaces, blonde hair slick, grinning hot—"Fuck, E"—my hands snag her waist underwater, her nails rake my shoulders slow—her breath brushes my ear—"Willa's losing it"—I laugh rough—"Fuck her"—phone buzzes on the deck, Willa's name flickering—ignored—Kayla's heat coils tight, my pulse roaring wild.

Water laps steady—Kayla's thighs graze mine, slick under the pool's blue shimmer—sun torches down, waves glinting sharp—her lips tease close, cherry bursting hot in my mouth—fuck yeah—my hands clamp her hips, yanking her tight—bruises kick alive—her nails trace my scars slow, tension coiling thick. Then Willa storms in—gate crashes wide—red hair blazes under noon glare, black boots stomping grass—her eyes sear—"You with him?"—voice slashes raw. She's laced up—denim skirt, top hugging tight—charges straight into the pool, diving hard—water erupts, boots splashing heavy. Kayla shrieks—"Willa!"—Willa snags her ponytail, yanking fierce—blonde strands rip—Kayla thrashes—"Get off!"—claws rake Willa's cheek, red streaks blooming. Willa hauls her out—water churns wild—Kayla's legs flail—Willa's soaked, boots sloshing—"You'll both pay!"—hex roars—her glare hits me—"Fuck you, Ethan!"—she shoves Kayla down, stomping off, dripping dark—my grin twists—"Fuck yeah"—Kayla pants, bruises throb—pool stills—Willa's curse cuts deep.

Water beads on Kayla's skin—my phone buzzes—Jayden's name flares—"Yo, E—where's my coke, you thieving fuck?"—his drawl cracks me up—my grin widens, coke from last night heavy in my pocket, silver paper crumpled. I laugh rough—"Fuck off, J"—text flies back—Kayla's "What's up?"—brushes soft—my edge sparks—"Jayden's whining for his stash"—her giggle's light—"Fuck him"—her heat hums—Willa's rage lingers—Jayden's spark flickers—my pulse pounds—fuck yeah.

Next day dawns gray—Nikes scuff school halls, bruises pulsing raw from David's fists—Kayla's pool brawl echoes, her nails, Willa's boots—split lip stings under harsh lights. Willa's there—red hair spilling wild, black boots carving tile—her eyes hit me, ice-cold, no hex, just a blade-sharp stare slicing me to nothing—fuck yeah, she's ghosting. My phone's dead silent since her "You're fucked" roared—Kayla slides in—"Hey, E"—cheer skirt swishing, voice soft—Willa's head turns slow, locking Kayla—chill, wordless, witchy frost burning quiet.

Lockers hum—Kayla's heat presses close—Willa stalks past, boots thudding, no glance—her stare flicks once, cutting deep—Kayla giggles—"She's pissed"—I smirk—"Fuck her"—but Willa's ice bites harder—no texts, no hex—silence screams where her fire used to blaze—my edge twists—Kayla's "What's her deal?"—lands light—Willa's void stings—phone stays mute—her steps fade—bruises throb—Kayla pulls—Willa seeds—fuck yeah.

Afternoon drags thick—school fades as I skate home, sun dipping low, board grinding under Nikes—Kayla's pool kiss burns hot, her nails raking, Willa's "You're fucked" ringing—phone buzzes sharp—I pull it, bruised knuckles flexing—Kayla's "We're done"—cuts quick, clean—my grin curls—"Why?"—I tap slow—her reply snaps—"You and Willa—too fucked up"—I laugh low, chaos my fuel—"Sure?"—her "Yeah—sorry E"—lands final—my lip stings, smirk widens—"Fuck it"—send "Cool"—Kayla's cherry fades—Willa's ice holds—phone quiets—rage simmers—fuck yeah—stakes shift.

Dusk settles heavy—Kayla's breakup stings faint as I skate, Nikes gripping, bruises pulsing—phone buzzes warm—Willa's "Come over"—pulls soft, urgent—I kick harder, streets blurring, wind tearing my hair wild—her witch house looms, clapboard peeling under last light—I drop my board, boots creaking up porch steps—Palo Santo chokes thick through the cracked door—I push in, stairs groaning as I climb, sage and wax curling heavy.

Willa sprawls on her bed—black lace clings tight, red hair spilling like fire over pillows, candlelight dancing—tarot cards sit still, Death card hidden—she looks up—"Hey, E"—voice low, witchy—my grin twists—"Hey, witch"—bruises throb as she rises, barefoot, toes

62 JUDE LUCAS

brushing wood—"Kayla's out—promised to stay gone—let's try again"—her words pull steady—my pulse kicks—fuck yeah—her heat nears—I step in—"She dumped me"—voice rough—Willa nods—"Good"—fingers trace my bruises, sage filling my lungs—her hex coils soft—we're back.

Night drops full—moon glows silver through her balcony door—we slip out, air cool—Willa leans on the railing, lace shimmering—her hair gleams red, eyes glinting—"Still dream of killing?"—voice threads soft, witchy—I grin, leaning close—"Yeah—why?"—low, steady—her lips curl—"Just asking"—my edge sharpens—fuck yeah—moonlight pools—she pulls me in—sheets tangle—her hands grip my waist—lace peels—my shirt rips—nails claw my bruises—lust cuts hot—mid-shag, her breath hits my ear—"Kill Kayla"—seductive, hex flaring—my pulse roars—"Fuck yeah"—I growl—her heat surges—Kayla's ghost sparks—shagging peaks—Willa's fire burns—murder hums alive.

She shifts—sheets slide—voice dips—"Jayden's shrooms—let's take Kayla to the woods"—eyes blaze, red hair wild—my grin curls—"Fuck yeah"—coke's echo flares, shrooms glow dark—Kayla's "We're done" fades—Willa's hex tightens—woods chaos seeds—my edge cuts—fuck yeah—night's stakes soar—her witchy trap coils—I'm in—moonlight dims—murder waits.

Woods & Shrooms

Dawn cracks the sky as we meet the girls at Clayboy's road—light's creeping up, pale and hazy. I lead, boots crunching gravel, backpack heavy—snacks, drinks, something sharp tucked deep. Clay's ahead, cutting through the quiet neighborhood, Willa and Kayla trailing—Willa's voice hums low, witchy, Kayla's laugh slicing through, sharp and bright. They're already at it, trading barbs under their breath—triangle's live, sparking early.

We push through pines—narrow paths, ducking branches, no usual hangout today. My secret spot's calling—towering trees, rocks underfoot. Kayla stumbles, crashes into me—her shorts brush my jeans, body warm against mine—my pulse kicks hard—fuck yeah—then Willa's there, peeling her off, her grip firm, eyes glinting hex. Single file now, pines close in—breeze hisses through needles, woods swallowing us. The clearing opens—moss and pine needles underfoot, a big-ass oak hulking center, branches twisting a canopy overhead. Clay drops the blanket, I roll a blunt—my ritual—group sinks in, waiting for the high.

Willa slides between my legs, back against my chest—her heat's possessive, staking claim. Pine and earth hit my nose—blunt sparks, smoke curling as I pass it—Clay's up, bouncing—"Yo! Shrooms, bro!"—his cap tilts, grin wild. I laugh—"Easy, animal"—but he's right, it's why we're here. Kayla digs into her bag, tosses plastic baggies onto the blanket—shrooms spill out, brittle, dark. Clay snags one, chomps—face twists, gagging—"Fuck!"—Willa shoves him a drink, we crack up as he chugs, choking it down—"You're a beast, bro"—my voice rough, grinning.

I dump half a bag in my palm, toss it back—nasty, bitter grit coats my tongue—pocket the rest. Willa and Kayla split one—Kayla's eyes flick me, teasing—Clay cuts the quiet—"Hope Jayden didn't swipe these from his mom's garden"—girls laugh, bright and sharp—I smirk—"Fuck yeah"—we kick back, impatient. Clay grumbles—"Nada yet"—Kayla's up—"Five minutes, chill! Let's walk!"—her spark shifts us—woods call—high's coming.

We head deeper, leaves crunching—Willa lets out a belly laugh, wild and loud—Clay and Kayla pile in, and I'm rolling too, ribs aching—fuck yeah, good pain.

Willa points—"Earth's breathing!"—we dive to look—ground swells, shrinks, alive. Kayla shouts—"No freaking way!"—her voice cuts sharp. Clay humps a tree, grinning like an idiot—we crack up—leaves flutter down, waving, breathing too. I drop flat under it—limbs light, tingling head to toe—Willa's next to me, red hair spilling—"This is perfect"—her voice hums, witchy, eyes wide. I grab her hand—fuck yeah—her heat's mine.

Kayla's up, dancing—arms wide, colors trailing, pulsing wild—shrooms twist it vivid—I can't look away. Heat hits my neck—Willa's eyes lock mine, burning—fuck, possessive as hell—"Your eyes set my skin on fire"—I quip, rough—Clay laughs—Willa doesn't flinch, just twirls up with Kayla—trance pulls me in.

Kayla's phone's out, recording—Willa spins, Clay somersaults, I laugh hard—Jayden's DM pings: *"Ayo, tell Ethan he better give me back my bag. Man thinks he can jack my stuff? He tweaking. Imma need it ASAP."* We lose it—Kayla's straight—"He's not bad"—we laugh harder. Clay rolls—"What, big dick?"—I grin—"You peeked that package, bro?"—hysterics hit—fuck yeah.

Clay's antsy—"Move!"—I'm with him, stumbling to the pond—rocks trip us, shrooms kicking hard—we hit a perch, water shimmering below. Breeze cuts the haze—a dragonfly zips past, wings glinting—Clay's voice echoes—"True story, you're the best friend I'll ever have." Hits me hard—no one's solid like him. "Doesn't matter which girl, I got your back—bros for life." Fist bump seals it—fuck yeah—time twists, surreal.

Back at the clearing, Willa's tense, scribbling hard—Kayla's staring, brows tight—quiet's thick, weird. I hook Spotify to Kayla's speaker—beats drop—I grab Willa's hand—she takes it, we dance—her close, I kiss her neck, claiming—Clay's arm's around Kayla—tension hums—fuck yeah.

We sprawl on pine needles, staring up—clouds twist into a math teacher's scowl, a bunny's flop, a dragon's snarl, a rose bleeding red—I slam my eyes shut, colors exploding wild behind lids, shrooms humming hot through me—fuck yeah kicks alive. "Damn, I'm so fucking high," I rasp low—eyes rip open, jolting me up, the big tree towering, leaves twitching like they're shroomed-out, breathing. "Ethan!"—Jayden's growl cuts the haze—"Where's my fucking bag, bro?"—he's there, popping outta the blur, face twisting mean and real as hell staggers into my trip.

Others' eyes bug wide—Jayden's blade flashes sharp in his grip, moonlight licking steel as he wobbles closer, boots crunching needles. "Where's my stash, Ethan?"—his drawl snaps nasty—heart slams my ribs, sweat dripping cold—"Chill, bro," I scrape out, voice rough, legs glued to the dirt—ground's got me, pinned—fingers claw slow for my switchblade, too fucking high to move fast. Jayden's on me—knife jams my neck, steel biting hot—fuck yeah flares wild, shroom haze swirling, can't fight, don't care.

"I ain't messin'—you'll bleed for steppin' to me," he snarls, breath stinking sour—vision melts, colors bleeding fuzzy—"Take it easy, Jayden," I mutter, blade digging deeper, warm and alive—his voice booms deep—"So fucking high on my shrooms, huh?"—I'm floating, not scared, heat wrapping me—"Waste of space, ain't even listenin'!"—he spits, knife twitching electric. "Stop it," Kayla slices through—steps in hard, blonde hair flashing in my swirl—"Calm down, Jay—put that shit away," she bites sharp, voice cutting my fog—"He's a jerk, stole my stash—dangerous fuck," Jayden growls—knife slides, sparking my skin—I squirm, buzzing alive—"You've got the blade, not him—chill with me," she shoves, her push landing firm—Jayden's eyes flicker, red and hazy, then he drops it, pocketing the steel—fuck yeah hums hot, high still owning me.

High as hell, I flop against the tree—bark claws my palms, tingling sharp as my legs hit the ground, floating loose in the shroom haze—colors slam wild, reds and greens bleeding, fuck yeah sparking hot through my veins. Eyes slam shut—vision crashes in—Willa and Kayla dancing, shirts ripped off, bras flashing, tumbling hot and twisted into the dirt—Willa's on her, lips crashing, my shadow smirking by the tree, stuck as fuck, legs numb, can't move—shroomed-out me grins dark, mocking my ass—fuck.

Kayla's head jerks—blood pours, scarlet streaming from her eyes, her mouth gaping—"Help me, Ethan!"—her scream rips through, heart slamming my ribs—vision flickers, leg twitching hard as I jolt up, Willa's grip clamping my hand tight—Clay's laugh cuts—"You were gone, bro"—sweat beads cold on my neck—"Fuck, he cut me!"—gash burns my arm, hot and raw—Willa's voice rolls cool—"Not deep, I cleaned it"—fuck yeah hums, shrooms still buzzing me alive.

I stagger up, floating shaky—drop next to Clay, legs jelly—Jayden's slumped beside him, staring cold, red eyes drilling me as the girls huddle under a tree, shadows curling around them. "My shrooms hit hard—you were fucked," Jayden drawls, downing his beer slow—"Arm's rough, you're a jerk, but we're similar, bro"—his voice cuts low, steady—I glare, squinting through the haze—"How the fuck?"—"Bougie 'burbs ain't us—both chasing Kayla—you're shady, she's your girl's BFF—I see everything," he says, eyes bulging wild—"Everything, Ethan." "Galaxies away," I snarl—rage pumps hot—I lurch to Willa and Kayla, boots dragging, sit hard—glance back—his candle tat stares, flame flickering in my shroomed-out skull—fuck yeah.

"What you eyeing?" he growl's—"Nothing, your ink," I snicker, voice thick—"Why the candle?"—shrooms pass hand to hand—"Not a dick—juvie shit, light guides me," he mutters—my side-eye cuts—"Prison'd make you a wifey"—his fist smacks my shoulder, playful but hard—Willa slices in—"Let's get tattoos!"—snags her marker, grin flashing—"Not a dick, Willa," I rasp—she draws fast, steps back—"Don't be silly, E"—bloody knife stains my forehead, Jayden's diamond gleams, Clay's weed leaf sprawls, Willa's witch hat spikes, Kayla's pentagram glows—fuck yeah roars through me, shroom haze sealing the marks.

Sunset slams wild—orange and purple explode, sky twisting like a shroomed-out fever as I flop onto the grass, sun bleeding low—alone now, ditched hard. Voices scream in my skull—friends gone—Kayla's with Jayden, Willa's hate burns, Clay's checked out—useless fucking loser—fuck rips through me, raw and hot.

Eyes clamp shut—fractals swirl, jagged and bright—voices won't quit, clawing my brain—I yell hoarse—"Clay! Willa!"—trees choke it dead. Kayla's laugh slices the haze—hers, sharp—pulls me hard—I call her, phone buzzing nothing—push through branches, thorns snagging—there she is, curls bouncing, Jayden's hands digging into her shorts, her neck locked in his grip—rage pumps red—I grab his collar, rip him off—fuck yeah surges, alive.

"Whoa, Ethan!"—he barks—Jayden smirks greasy—"Back up, dawg"—I spin on him—"Why you even here, Jayden?"—my shout tears my throat—he steps in—"She sent me the pin," he mutters, eyes blank—Kayla nods—"Yeah, I did"—I glare at her—"He tried to stab me!"—Jayden snaps—"Watch it!"—I shove hard—"Shut the fuck up!"—Kayla shoves past—"Grow up"—she's gone, vanishing into the dusk—fuck stabs my chest.

"You think you can have 'em both? You're nothing—they'll dip," Jayden taunts, voice dripping slime—he pulls a cigarette —"Light, bro?"—that smirk snaps me, brain splintering—"Shut the fuck up!"—I lunge, knife sinking fast into his neck, steel biting deep—confusion twists his face, eyes popping wide—I slash again, tearing flesh open—fuck yeah roars hot, blood gushing warm over my hand—not hard at all. He staggers, choking wet—pathetic—grabs air, legs buckling—I yank him back, his weight sagging—slash one more, neck gaping—drops heavy, eyes bulging dead—blood pools dark, soaking dirt—I kick his limp ass, boots thudding—dead as fuck—drag him slow, arms heavy, into the bushes—leaves crunch, body slumps hidden—loot his weed, shrooms, blade—fuck yeah, I'm king.

I stride off—superhero high—hit the pond, clean the blade slow in the murk, blood swirling red then gone—pocket it, steel cool against my thigh—Kayla's by the fire now, alone, tranced out, flames licking her curls—I sit quiet, pulse pounding wild—fucking fantastic—erased him, he's nothing—I'm everything—brain fragments, fuck yeah reigning, king shit pulsing through every cracked piece.

"Where's Jayden?" Kayla asks—her voice cuts my high, sharp through the fire's crackle—I lock eyes with the flames, grin twisting—"Went home, too messed up—said goodbye." She squints, puzzled—fuck her doubt, it stabs me—brain fragments tighter, buzzing wild.

"I'll call him"—shit, his phone's buried with him in the bush—I grab her shoulders hard—"Check my cut!"—shove my arm in her face, gash pulsing red—wild laugh tears outta me, high pitching—stumble forward, crash on her—our laughs smash together, hers soft, mine unhinged—Jayden's gone, erased—fuck yeah roars hot in my chest.

She pulls back slow—"Sorry about him—stupid, tripping," she mutters, eyes soft—my wicked grin splits wide—"Killing him wasn't a mistake"—words slip dark, sharp—"No need—he's gone"—smirk locks tight, brain splintering, high still kinging me—her doubt fades, can't touch me.

"You I wanted—to kiss," she says, hand reaching slow—stops mid-air—Willa and Clay roll up, shadows swaying—Willa's voice hums—"Interrupt?"—deep in the shrooms, eyes glassy—fuck yeah flares, she's mine again—Clay flops beside us—"See colors, wild shit"—grinning loose—Willa whispers—"Amazing"—her arm slides around me—I yank her close—"Walk," I growl—fuck yeah pulses raw.

We hit a tree—bark claws my hands as I press her hard against it, rough trunk biting her back—Jayden's body slumps close, hidden in the bushes, blood stink curling faint—my hands grip her waist, lace ripping—hard and fast, her nails claw my neck—voices scream in my skull, won't fucking stop—fuck yeah drowns 'em, shagging her wild with him rotting right there—king shit reigns, brain cracking wide.

Night rolls thick—vodka and shrooms pass hand to hand, flames licking in the dark—Willa cuts through the haze—"Blood magick's power—unbreakable bond"—her voice hums low, witchy—fuck yeah sparks hot in my chest.

Fire carves her face sharp—eyes lock us four, glinting fierce—"Bond us forever," she says—Kayla's voice trembles—"How?"—fuck twists my gut, psycho itch waking.

"Cut our palms—blood mixes—bound beyond death," Willa murmurs, steady and dark—Clay balks, shifting—"Too fucking intense"—she leans in—"Stronger than life"—my grin flares—"For sure!"—itch burns wild, fuck yeah clawing alive.

Clay shrugs—"Okay, guess so"—Willa's eyes hit me—"Knife, E—you always have it"—smirk curls her lips—fuck yeah roars—I snap the blade open, steel flashing in the firelight.

"Cut me," Willa says, palm out—whispers soft—"Want this?"—"Damn straight," I growl—slash her quick, red line blooming—Kayla's palm shakes—"Hurt?"—"Yeah," she breathes—I cut, blood welling—she whimpers low, urge flaring hot—fuck pulses hard.

They lock hands, blood smearing—my smirk twists—I grab Clay's wrist—"Shut up, baby"—cut fast, blood dripping—he grunts—our palms slap together, red mixing—Kayla whispers—"Eternity"—fuck yeah hums electric through me.

Willa's lips crash mine—palms press, blood warm—she grabs Kayla, kisses her deep—red streaks her cheek—pulls me in—kisses flare wild—Clay joins, his hand tracing Kayla's stomach, slow and hungry—fuck yeah ignites, heat surging.

Clothes rip—naked now—Clay's on Willa, moans spilling—I bury into Kayla, electric jolts ripping through—fuck yeah owns me—shift to Willa—"Bonded forever," she gasps, voice threading the dark—Kayla's lips hit mine—move back to her—fuck yeah reigns wild.

She gasps—"Ethan"—body trembling under me—I'm on top—her eyes bulge, scream tearing out—knife slams her shoulder—Willa's behind her, stabbing savage—neck next, blood spurting—Kayla claws air, screams shredding—fuck—hallucinating?—brain fragments, shrooms twisting.

Willa lifts my knife high—stabs again, brutal—Clay roars loud—rips her off, gripping hard—knife streams blood, dripping red in the firelight—fuck yeah pulses, king shit cracking wild through my skull.

Kayla sobs hard—blood pours hot from her shoulder, her neck—Clay's got Willa pinned, arms locked tight—I yank Jayden's blade from my pocket, steel glinting red—jump fast—"Help me!" she begs, voice cracking wet—fuck twists my gut, high roaring.

Heart slams wild—"Let go!" I snarl—"You kidding me!?" Clay snaps back, grip tight—Willa nods slow, eyes dark—Kayla gurgles—"Help"—blood bubbles—my voice cuts calm—"Let go, help her"—Clay's hold loosens, he kneels—I lunge, stab his neck deep—blade sinks, hot—slash his back—he gasps sharp—Kayla bolts, staggering—fuck yeah flares, king shit alive.

"Fun!" I roar—throw the blade hard—it slams her leg, she drops—struggles up, invincible—chase kicks in, boots pounding—she trips over Jayden's corpse, screams ripping—his dead eyes stare—I grab her ankles, yank her down—fuck yeah surges, brain cracking wild.

"Running where?"—voice thunders—press her hard into the dirt, face grinding mud—pull the blade free, cut her collar deep—blood gushes warm, scream shredding air—she writhes, thrashing—I flip her rough—knees pin her chest—eyes lock mine, wide and wet—my grin splits—stab her stomach, steel tearing—fuck yeah hums electric.

Stand slow—blood drips thick from my hands—her sobs choke, wet gasps—yank her hair, force her to kneel—"Why?" she rasps, voice breaking—"Shh," I hiss—stab her chest hard—blade crunches bone—she convulses, body jerking—eyes lock mine, fading fast—surge hits wild—"I'm everything," I growl—her lights go out—fuck yeah crowns me, king of the dark.

After Party

Head back staring at the stars—my stomach twists, churning hard—I puke, gasping ragged—nothing's left, gut hollow—fuck yeah slams me, raw and sharp.

Anxiety crashes wild—I sink back, trembling bad—Kayla's lifeless body sprawls there—pale lips parted, wounds gaping—blood cakes her, thick and dark—fuck twists me—I brush her hair soft, fingers shaking—wipe blood from her cheek—kiss her cold forehead—adrenaline buzzes hot—I lie beside her, grab her limp hand—fuck yeah burns, electric and wrong.

Bad trip won't fade—heart pounds wild—I lurch up, knife gripped tight—body shakes—"Willa! Clayton!"—scream tears out—"Where the fuck are you?"—fuck echoes—search frantic—they're gone—Jayden's face looms close—swollen blue, blood pooling under him—dead eyes scream—fuck yeah cuts, raw and real.

Panic surges fast—knife shakes in my hand—genius sparks—I frame Jayden, scapegoat king—toss his blade beside him, steel clinking dirt—fuck, I stumble back to Kayla—her body's still, cold as hell—redress her slow, hands steady—carry her, dead weight heavy—set her by him, eyes wide and empty—fire pit glows faint—I snag my knife, plant it with Jayden—fuck yeah hums, it's fucking perfect.

Pond shimmers dark—I shiver hard, step in—water swallows me, cold biting deep—woods hum low—fuck, adrenaline dips—I dunk my head, hold it under—climb out slow, dripping—yank clothes on, soaked and tight—reality slams down—fuck yeah, I'm free, king shit alive.

Willa and Clay vanished—did I kill him?—snitch me out?—mind races wild—I yell—"Willa!"—woods choke it dead—stumble fast, legs jelly—sprint harder—outrun the dark—hit home—fuck yeah, I'm safe, pulse roaring.

Shakes hit on the porch—open the door slow—keep it quiet—fuck, I'm cool—floor creaks soft—stairs snap loud—fuck yeah echoes, brain splintering.

Bathroom looms—I strip quick—toss clothes in a pile—colors flare hard—tiles gleam under light—cloth glows red, blood-soaked—fuck, I shower—steam chokes thick—warmth jolts me—water slicks tiles—Kayla's scent clings, cherry faint—Willa's sage mixes in—frenzy flashes—kisses burn hot—over her—Jayden's corpse—screams rip—blood spills—I stab Clay—stab Kayla—fuck yeah haunts, wild and cracked.

Blood stains my tee—hoodie's fucked too—dry off rough—scrub 'til it fades—hide the mess deep—fuck, I crawl into bed—call Willa—no pickup—text sharp—"Where are you?"—fuck yeah pulses, waiting tense.

Can't sleep—night replays brutal—where's Clay?—Willa?—body aches raw—sun creeps up—room stays dark—fuck, blood stinks—pine, vape—Kayla's screams echo loud—sirens wail close—bangs hit the door—heart slams hard—I'm fucked up—right here—fuck yeah ends, king shit crowned.

Come Down

Door creaks open—I step back fast—heart slams wild as two detectives loom—one leans on the car, smoke curling, the other towers over me—messy hair, red nose glaring—his badge reads "McBride." "Morning," McBride grunts, eyes pinning me—Mom's hand clamps my shoulder—"Something wrong?"—her voice shakes.

McBride shifts to her—"Your son's friends got hurt—Willa and Clay, found in the woods, stabbed up bad"—Mom gasps sharp, grip digging—"Are they okay?"—he nods, eyes sliding back—"Think he was there"—my mind spins—Willa stabbed?—fuck, did I hurt her?—her witchy smirk flashes—fuck yeah twists—brain cracks—"Questions, Ethan—were you?"—David steps up—"Moment alone," he says firm, staring McBride down.

McBride dips his head—"Take your time"—door slams—David's slap stings my cheek—eyes bore in—"What's going on?"—I shut my eyes—words could save—"Fuck," I mutter—brain twists.

"Woods went bad—Jayden stabbed Kayla and Clay, creepy shit—I saved her, got cut"—show my arm, gash red—"He lost it"—David's voice cuts—"Why no cops?"—I stammer—"Weed, shrooms—didn't know"—Mom's stare burns—"Why not us?"—"Scared," I rasp—fuck churns hot.

David hauls McBride back—he sinks into a chair, gaze drilling—"Left them bleeding, showered, slept?"—disdain bites—I shrug—"Tripping hard, phones rang—no answer"—he spots my forehead—"What's that?"—panic spikes—Willa's knife drawing—fuck.

"Just drawings," I blurt—Mom reaches—McBride blocks—"Evidence"—her tremble cracks—"For what?"—David slams the wall—"No—lawyer!"—fuck yeah flares.

McBride stares hard—"Okay, waiting"—silence drops—Mom weeps soft—David paces—my eyes hit the floor—fuck yeah steadies me.

Jacobs strides in—suit sharp, cutting the mess—sits close while McBride's crumpled shirt and bloodshot eyes glare—fuck—I spill the woods, McBride fires questions—Jacobs cuts in—"Fifth"—fuck yeah owns it, king shit tight.

McBride paces outside—phone buzzes—neighbors gawk, Mrs. Fish with her poodle, Fletcher sipping coffee—Jacobs talks low—returns, hands on my shoulders—eyes dead on—"Station soon, I'm there"—fuck yeah trusts—McBride recites rights, voice flat—gawkers stare—Mom sobs, trailing David's car—fuck weighs heavy.

Car creeps slow—silence chokes—I stare out—lawns mowed neat, dogs trot, girls walk, coffees clutched—fuck—head throbs—body trembles—I feel like shit—fuck yeah glares, holding me up.

Stop jolts—puke hits pavement—McBride hauls me into a cramped room—Mom trembles, tears wet—Jacobs leans, notebook out—David asks—"Okay?"—I mumble—"Yeah," shaky—fuck—Jacobs breaks it—"Charges or home soon"—Mom grips me—"You wouldn't hurt"—David's quiet—fuck yeah sticks—silence waits—I keep cool—fuck burns steady.

Door slams open—bang rattles my bones—McBride storms in—boots thud hard, eyes lock mine, prickling—"Two bodies—Jayden and Kayla—both gone," he growls, voice rough—stomach twists sharp—fuck yeah steadies—"Kayla, no way," I mutter—hands shove my face, fingers digging—lips twist—fuck spins the lie—psycho mask locks tight.

McBride glares cold—"Friends took a hit—two didn't make it"—words sink heavy—chest hums—fuck yeah bites—"Willa and Clay next, when docs clear—stay," he adds—boots scrape out—Mom and David nod fast—his head tilts me—door clicks—fuck holds—breath steadies—"Jayden fucked them—I saved her," I hiss inside—psycho lie burns—Willa's nod flashes—fuck yeah trusts—fire flares—fuck snarls low.

Head throbs—Willa's face flickers—did I?—fuck twists—leg kicks, chair creaks—breath rasps—psycho edge hums—fuck yeah glares—"Gotta get out," I mutter—fuck cuts—David's boots scuff—coffee stinks—Jacobs' pen scratches—leg jumps—room chokes—fuck yeah reigns—psycho fire burns—fuck snarls steady.

[Tayla] "Girl we saw Ethan in a cop car fr "

[Mandy] "Omg no way I can't believe this!! "

[Rayne] "Always knew he was weird af tbh"

[Maya] "Lol Rayne u were tryna make out w him all the time "

[Rayne] "Yea he's hot but super weird lol"

[Mandy] "They lookin for Kayla, idk where she at. Willa & Clayton in hospital. Hope she not dead omg "

[Rayne] "What if he killed her fr"

[Maya] "We saw Kayla & Ethan at the pier that one time"

[Rayne] "Omfg yea they were suckin face so hard "

[Maya] "Why hot guys always crazy lol"

[Maxine] "This is so disrespectful to Kayla & me. Plz stop til we know more. I'm legit devastated rn "

[Tayla] "Ik girl, I'm here for u. Bet Kayla's fine tho"

[Rayne] "Ethan looked hot in that cop car tho lmao

EVIDENCE

Case: Homicide—Kayla [REDACTED], Jayden [REDACT-ED]Date: July 14, 2024Officer: Det. Peter McBride

Summary:

July 14, 2024, 06:34—Gladys Drive woods—Mavis and Peter Strober report two wounded. Willa [REDACTED], abdominal laceration, conscious. Clayton [REDACTED], neck and back wounds, semi-conscious—minors, no ID, no phones. Paramedics transport—stable. 10:24—search team finds deceased: Kayla [REDACTED], unclothed, supine, arms crossed—multiple sharp force injuries: hands, arms, neck, back, chest. Items: vape, phone, towel, Nike trainers. Jayden [REDACTED], lateral position, two neck wounds. Items: wallet, $700, phone, 3 cannabis bags, 4 psilocybin bags, two blood-marked switchblades. Pronounced dead—10:28—Det. McBride.

Items Seized—367 Forterbaine Rd (Ethan [REDACTED]):

- Hoodie, blue—blood-like stains on sleeves

- Photograph—Kayla [REDACTED], slashed, bodily fluids

- Nike trainers—match crime scene footprints

- Cannabis—0.5 grams

- Psilocybin—1 gram

- Switchblades—4

Witness—Willa [REDACTED]:

"Ethan [REDACTED]—boyfriend, two years. Kayla—friend since age 4—caught with Ethan at pool, ended it. He begged, threatened harm—blood fixation, knife incidents. Woods, 14/7/2024—intoxicated: mushrooms, cannabis, vodka. [REDACTED] stabbed Kayla, back—she resisted. Clayton intervened, stabbed—me, stomach. He chased Kayla—hid, heard screams. Phones lost—passed out, found on road. [REDACTED]'s knife—Jayden absent."

Witness—Clayton [REDACTED]:

"Ethan—friend, 7 years—owns knives, said he'd kill one day—fights often. Woods, 14/7/2024—drugs: mushrooms, cannabis, alcohol. Jayden clashed—Kayla stopped—memory impaired post-incident."

Charges—Ethan [REDACTED] (DOB: 8/12/2007):

- Second-degree murder—Kayla [REDACTED]

- Second-degree murder—Jayden [REDACTED]

- Attempted murder—Willa [REDACTED]

- Attempted murder—Clayton [REDACTED]

Note:

Investigation ongoing—[REDACTED] presumed innocent until adjudicated.

Juvie Drop

Head throbs hard—Willa's alive, Clay too—fuck twists my gut deep—leg kicks wild, chair creaks loud under me—psycho calm flares hot—"Gotta play this smart," I mutter low—fuck yeah glares steady, holding me tight. McBride's boots stomp heavy—door bangs open wide, rattling my skull—red nose flares ugly, eyes burn into me—"Clayton can't remember a damn thing—Willa says it's you, Ethan—not Jayden," he growls, voice rough as gravel—my chest locks tight—fuck—Willa's nod flashes cruel, her witchy smirk turning sour—brain splinters sharp, she fucking framed me—fuck yeah burns hot into rage.

"Two bodies—Jayden, Kayla—dead," he snaps cold—Mom chokes hard, hands slapping her mouth—David pales fast, face dropping—Jacobs sits still, suit crisp and cool—my hands shove my face—"No fucking way," I rasp, voice cracking sharp—psycho grin twists inside me—lie's a blade, dulled by her hex—fuck snarls wild and raw. "Your friends got hit—two didn't make it," McBride says, heavy as lead—chest hums tight—"Jayden fucked 'em—I saved her,"

I hiss low—Willa's betrayal stabs deep—fuck yeah trusts nothing now—king shit cracks, fury roaring steady through me.

"Cuffs," McBride snaps—metal clanks loud—two uniforms step in, grab my arms rough—chains bite my wrists, cold and tight—I grin wide—"Easy, boys," voice rough but steady—Mom sobs sharp—"Ethan!"—David's fist slams the table—"Lawyer stays!"—Jacobs nods firm—"I'm with him"—McBride snarls—"Move"—they yank me up hard—boots scuff concrete—fuck yeah holds strong—psycho edge hums alive—Mom's tears drip, David's glare fades—station blurs as they haul me out—sun slams my eyes—fuck—puke burns my throat, shrooms sour—I swallow it down—king shit reigns tall.

Squad car waits—black and white, lights dead—door swings open—uniform shoves me in—cuffs dig deeper into skin—Jacobs slides beside me—"Keep quiet," his suit's sharp, voice low and calm—McBride climbs up front—"Juvie run"—engine growls low—fuck—tires bite asphalt—lawns blur past, girls freeze with coffees—my grin curls slow—psycho fire flares hot—fuck yeah owns the ride—windows hum soft, wind slips through—king shit vibes steady—cuffs clank with every bump—Jacobs scribbles fast—"Self-defense angle—Jayden's the psycho"—I nod—"Fuck yeah"—lie's locked tight—Willa's nod hums bitter—woods blood flashes quick—Kayla's "Why?"—Jayden's neck—Clay's gasp—fuck cuts sharp through me.

Car slows—juvie looms ahead—gray block, razor wire glinting mean—gates creak open—uniform hauls me out—boots hit gravel hard—fuck—air's thick, stale—McBride stomps ahead—"Intake"—metal door bangs loud—hall echoes—fluorescent buzz stabs my skull—cuffs clank—psycho calm holds—"Name," some fat guard grunts—pen scratches—"Ethan," I say, voice rough and steady—fuck yeah owns it—"Strip," he points—boots off, jeans drop—orange jumpsuit slaps my chest—cuffs snap free, then clamp back—fuck—cell door clangs shut—concrete walls choke tight—king shit smirks quiet.

Bunk's hard—metal bites my back—I sprawl out, chains clinking soft—fuck—walls stare gray and blank—Kayla's ghost flickers faint—cherry vape, blood dripping—my grin twists slow—"Hey, Kayz," voice low—fuck yeah hums steady—psycho edge burns—guard bangs—"Quiet!"—I laugh rough—"Fuck you"—echo bounces—cell's tight, air's dead—Willa's nod glows—lie's gold—Jayden's the fall guy—fuck—head kicks back—bruises throb—woods high lingers—"I'm everything," mutter slips—king shit reigns—fuck yeah cuts deep.

Footsteps thud—guard's back—"Lawyer"—Jacobs steps in—suit sharp, eyes flat—"Plea's shaping—self-defense—Jayden's prints on the knife"—fuck—my grin curls—"Told you," voice rough—"Fuck yeah"—he nods—"Hold tight—court soon"—door clangs shut—fuck—cell locks—psycho fire flares—Kayla's eyes flash—blood pools—Willa's hex hums—fuck yeah owns it—king shit waits—juvie's a cage—I'm the beast—fuck cuts sharp.

Cell hums gray—bunk bites my back, chains clank soft—Kayla's ghost flickers, cherry vape dripping blood—my grin twists—"Miss me, Kayz?"—voice rough—fuck yeah hums low—psycho fire burns steady. Guard bangs—"Up, punk!"—boots thud—door swings wide—"Lawyer"—I swing off, Nikes scuffing concrete—fuck—cuffs snap tight—guard's meaty hand shoves—hall echoes—fluorescent buzz stabs—fuck yeah owns it—king shit strides—woods high lingers—"I'm everything," mutter slips—Willa's framing me—Clayton's blank—psycho edge cuts sharp.

Room's tight—metal table gleams—Jacobs waits, suit crisp, eyes flat—beside him, she's fire—hot assistant, curves and heat—black skirt hugs tight, blouse unbuttoned just enough—dark hair spills, lips red, eyes glinting sharp—fuck—my grin curls—"Hey, gorgeous," voice rough—she smirks—"Sit, Ethan"—Jacobs nods—"This is Mia—my paralegal"—fuck yeah—psycho hum flares—cuffs clank as I drop—boots kick up—"What's the play?"—king shit leans in—Mia's pen scratches—legs cross, skirt rides—fuck—woods blood flashes—Willa's nod—Clayton's haze—lie's cracking.

Jacobs cuts in—"Self-defense shaky—Jayden's prints hold, but Willa's pointing at you—Clayton's memory's gone"—fuck—my grin twists—"Willa's a liar—Clay's my bro, he'd back me"—voice rough—Mia's eyes flick—"Clayton can't—total blank"—fuck—psycho edge hums—Willa's hex stabs—Jacobs slides a tablet—"Court's online—today—plea's a gamble"—fuck—my pulse kicks—"How long?"—he leans—"Juvie, short—Willa's framing's thin, no proof yet"—Mia's lips curl—"Stay cool, Ethan"—fuck yeah—psycho fire flares—cuffs bite—"She's fucked me," mutter slips—king shit burns—Clayton's fog twists—fuck cuts deep.

Guard hauls me—chains rattle—screen room's stark—monitor glows—tablet hums—Jacobs and Mia flank me—judge pops up, face pinched—"Ethan, present"—voice drones—fuck—my grin holds—"Yeah," rough and steady—Mia's heat brushes close—perfume stings—fuck yeah—psycho fire hums—Jacobs nods—"Plea, Your Honor—self-defense—Jayden attacked—Willa's unreliable,

Clayton's amnesiac"—judge squints—"Evidence conflicts—Willa accuses, Clayton's void—Jayden's prints align"—fuck—my grin curls—"Willa's a witch"—voice low—lie's gold fraying—king shit reigns—fuck yeah trusts.

"Detention pending review," judge grunts—"Twenty-one days, juvenile facility—witness clarity needed"—gavel cracks—screen blanks—fuck—my grin twists—"Short leash," voice rough—Jacobs claps my shoulder—"Willa's play's weak—Clayton's key"—Mia's eyes glint—"No stunts, hero"—fuck yeah—psycho edge hums—guard yanks—"Back"—cuffs bite—boots scuff—hall echoes—cell looms—fuck—king shit smirks—"Twenty-one's mine," mutter slips—Willa's frame glows—Clayton's blank stings—woods high burns—fuck yeah owns it.

Cell clangs shut—bunk's cold—I sprawl out, chains off—Nikes kick up—fuck—walls choke tight, gray and dead—Mia's curves flash—red lips, tight skirt—fuck yeah—psycho fire twists—Willa's nod haunts—Clayton's haze blanks—Kayla's blood hums—lie's iron bends—twenty-one days—king shit laughs—"Willa's fucked," mutter slips—fuck cuts sharp.

Cell clangs—bunk's cold, concrete bites—twenty-one days crawl—Nikes scuff—fuck—Willa's frame glows, witchy hex coiling—Clayton's blank stabs, bro's fog a ghost—Kayla's blood hums, cherry vape fading—my grin curls—"Hey, Kayz"—voice rough—fuck yeah owns it—psycho fire simmers—guard bangs—"Move, punk!"—boots thud—door swings—guard's meaty paw yanks—"Therapist"—cuffs snap—chains bite—fuck—hall echoes—fluorescent buzz cuts—king shit strides—"Game on," mutter slips—psycho edge hums sharp.

Room's stark—white walls glare—one chair, one table—she's there—soft eyes, sage scent drifting—brown hair loose, bracelets jingle—fuck—my grin twists—"Who's this?"—voice rough—she stands—"I'm Jess—your therapist"—voice calm, steady—fuck—cuffs clank—guard shoves—I drop—boots kick up—"Hey, Jess—king shit's here"—rough and loud—fuck yeah—psycho hum flares—chains rattle—her pen hovers—"First session—how's juvie hitting you?"—sage wafts—fuck—my grin holds—"Like a throne—own it"—king shit burns—Jess sits—"Let's start easy—breathe with me"—fuck—bullshit's live.

"In slow—nose—hold—out mouth," she says—hands rise, fall—fuck—my eyes roll—"Seriously?"—voice rough—Jess nods—"Try it—calms the storm"—sage stings—fuck yeah—psycho edge twists—I lean—"Fine"—suck air—nose burns—hold—chest tight—blow out—lips crack—fuck—my grin curls—"Happy now?"—rough and sharp—her pen scratches—"Good—again"—fuck—in- hale—hold—exhale—bullshit hums—Willa's frame flashes—Clay- ton's blank—Kayla's ghost—fuck—king shit smirks—"This your fix?"—Jess tilts—"Your storm—what's churning?"—fuck—psycho fire simmers—lie's locked.

"Willa's screwing me—framing me—Clayton's blank—can't talk," I snap—voice cuts—fuck—cuffs bite—"Jayden went psycho—I saved her"—gold lie glows—Jess scribbles—"Willa's story—Clay- ton's fog—what's yours?"—eyes lock—fuck yeah—psycho hum holds—"Truth's mine—Jayden slashed, I stopped him—Willa's a liar, twisting shit"—voice rough—her pen scratches—"Stopped him how?"—fuck—my grin twists—"Fought—took a cut—hero shit"—arm flicks, Willa's sketch glows—fuck—Jess leans—"Cut

where?"—sage wafts—psycho edge hums—"Arm—see?"—rough
and steady—fuck yeah owns it.

"Breathe again—deep," she says—hands lift—fuck—inhale—hold—exhale—bullshit drags—my grin holds—"This
crap work?"—voice rough—Jess nods—"Helps—woods—what
happened?"—fuck—psycho fire flares—Willa's nod—Kayla's
blood—lie's iron—"Jayden flipped—knife out—slashed 'em—I
jumped—saved her"—fuck yeah—king shit burns—her pen scratches—"Saved her—then what?"—eyes glint—fuck—my grin curls—"I
stopped him—left 'em bleeding"—voice rough—Jess tilts—"You
left?"—fuck—psycho edge twists—"Tripping—shrooms—crashed
home"—lie's gold—fuck yeah holds.

"Feel that night?" she asks—sage stings—fuck—my
boots kick—"Yeah—chaos—Jayden's fault"—voice
cuts—Jess scribbles—"Chaos—yours?"—fuck—my grin
twists—"Nah—his—Willa's bullshit's the storm"—rough and
sharp—psycho hum flares—her pen stops—"Breathe—let
it settle"—fuck—inhale—hold—exhale—bullshit hums—Kayla's ghost fades—Willa's frame glows—Clayton's blank
stabs—fuck—king shit smirks—"Good?"—Jess nods—"For
now"—sage wafts—fuck yeah—psycho fire simmers—chains
clank—Guard bangs—"Time"—fuck—my grin holds—"Later,
Jess"—voice rough—king shit reigns—fuck cuts sharp.

Cell hums—bunk bites, concrete chills—Nikes scuff—fuck—Willa's
frame tightens, Clayton's blank haunts—Kayla's ghost fades—my
grin curls—"Still king"—voice rough—fuck yeah simmers—door
clangs—Jacobs steps in—suit crisp, eyes hard—"Ethan"—voice
cuts—fuck—my boots kick up—"What's up?"—rough and

steady—psycho hum flares—cuffs clank—he sits—"Bad news—DA's pushing—moving you to adult prison"—fuck—my grin twists—"Bullshit—why?"—voice snaps—king shit burns—Jacobs sighs—"Willa's story hardened—Clayton's still blank—evidence tilts—nothing I can do"—fuck—psycho edge stabs.

"Fight it," I growl—voice rough—fuck—cuffs bite—"Tried—judge ruled—transfer's set," he says—eyes drop—fuck yeah—my grin holds—"King shit owns any cage"—rough and loud—Jacobs nods—"Stay sharp—appeal's long"—fuck—psycho fire twists—door bangs—two guards storm—boots thud—"Up, punk"—Guard's growl—fuck—chains rattle—hands yank—cuffs snap tighter—shackles slam—feet locked, hands bound—metal bites deep—fuck—my grin curls—"Fancy jewelry"—voice rough—guards shove—hall echoes—Jacobs fades—"Hang on, Ethan"—fuck—king shit strides—shackles clank—psycho edge hums—adult prison looms—fuck yeah cuts sharp.

[Kyle_grainger]

kys

[Brad_904e]

fry in the electric chair

[Jake_quinton76]

They love pretty boys in prison

[CraigDewar]

I love my children, but if they did something like this, I would have to report them.

[Suzamarks]

Apple doesn't fall far from the tree...

[Jackiepartridge]

All this is PURE EVIL!

[Mandi Edwards]

I hope he gets bum raped every day and dies of covid and AIDS

[Casey543]

Why didn't the mother call the cops when he was little, I would have done that

[Elizabeth]

you wouldn't look cute even in an electric chair

[K. Taboo]

Ethan, I love you

[Perfectly.Charley]

don't worry guys, Jesus will deal with this one

BIG LEAGUES

Cell bites hard—bars hum low—stink claws at me—fuck—my grin curls wide as I pace the concrete, bare feet grinding cold—Nikes gone now—fuck yeah simmers steady—Willa's frame twists in my head—Clayton's blank haunts—Kayla's ghost flickers faint—fuck—I dig fingers into the wall—nails bite sharp—carve an "E," deep and jagged—my grin twists tighter—"Keeping demons busy," I mutter, voice rough—king shit burns hot—steps echo quick—bunk creaks—fist slams down—metal sings—psycho edge hums alive—fuck cuts sharp.

Chains slip off—hands flex free—fuck—fingers rake my hair, twisting hard—my grin holds—"Still me," I growl, voice rough—fuck yeah—wall's cold—nails claw again—"K" slashes deep—stink hums thick—piss and sweat—mind spins—woods flash—Kayla's "Why?"—Willa's nod—lie's gold—fuck—my grin curls—"Busy's king," I say, rough and sharp—pace quickens—scratch—pace—bunk groans under my fist—rhythm bites—psycho fire flares—fuck yeah owns it—cell's tight—king shit smirks—demons dance—fuck roars low.

Light flickers—shadows shift across—fuck—my grin twists—"Mine," I mutter, voice rough—nails dig slow—"A" carves into the wall—stink thickens—Kayla's blood hums faint—cherry fades—psycho edge burns steady—pace slows—fingers trace—"E-K-A" glows scratched—fuck—my grin holds—"Keeping 'em tame," I say, rough and low—fuck yeah—king shit reigns—cell's cold—bars sing soft—psycho fire simmers—fuck cuts deep—alone's sexy—fuck roars loud.

Cell hums gray—bars bite—stink claws—fuck—my grin curls—"King's den," I growl, voice rough—bare feet grip concrete—"E-K-A" scratches glow—fuck yeah simmers—Willa's frame twists—Clayton's blank stabs—Kayla's ghost hums—fuck—door clangs loud—boots thunder—shadow looms huge—big fucker fills the frame—gruff growl cuts—"You're the kid"—fuck—my grin twists—"Yeah, who's this?"—voice rough and sharp—king shit leans—psycho edge flares—fuck cuts deep.

He's massive—Ed—six-foot-plus, meat slab—shoulders bulge—gray uniform strains tight—badge glints—"Officer Pratt," he rumbles—fuck—face scarred—jaw square, eyes black—buzz cut bristles—gruff voice rolls—"Heard you're trouble"—fuck—my grin curls—"Heard right," I say, voice rough—bare feet shift—fuck yeah—psycho hum burns—he steps in—boots thud heavy—cell shrinks—stink thickens—piss, sweat, him—fuck—his grin cracks—"Cocky shit," rough and low—king shit smirks—"Damn straight"—fuck—psycho edge hums—sexy clash sparks.

"Woods kid—stabbed 'em, huh?"—Ed growls—eyes bore into me—fuck—my grin holds—"Jayden's mess—I saved her," I say, lie's gold—voice rough—fuck yeah—psycho fire flares—he looms closer—"Bullshit—Willa's singing, Clayton's mute"—fuck—my grin twists—"Willa's a witch—Clay's my bro"—voice rough and sharp—Ed's laugh barks—deep, raw—"Bro's fucked—blank slate"—fuck—king shit burns—"Still king," I snap—voice cuts—he steps nearer—breath stinks—coffee, smoke—fuck—psycho edge hums—"Size me up, kid," gruff and low—fuck yeah—sexy power kicks.

Eyes lock—his black, mine blue—fuck—my grin curls—"Big guy—slow guy?"—voice rough—Ed snarls—"Test me"—fuck—his fist flexes—meat hooks—fuck yeah—psycho fire twists—I lean in—"Bring it," I say, rough and sharp—king shit smirks—he grabs—shirt twists—lifts me—bars slam my back—fuck—my grin holds—"Strong—dumb?"—voice rough—Ed's eyes flare—"Smart mouth," gruff growl—fuck—psycho edge burns—his grip tightens—sexy clash hums—fuck yeah owns it.

"Rules here—my cage, my reign," he snaps—breath hits sour—fuck—my grin twists—"King shit bows to no one," I growl, voice rough—fuck—Ed shoves—bars bite hard—psycho fire flares—"You'll break," gruff and low—fuck yeah—my grin curls—"Try me"—voice rough and sharp—he drops me—feet slap concrete—fuck—king shit stands tall—"Fun start," I say, voice cuts—Ed's grin cracks—"Fresh meat's bold"—fuck—psycho edge hums—his boots shift—fuck yeah—sexy power twists—cell locks tight—king shit burns.

"Chow's soon—move when I say," he growls—eyes bore—fuck—my grin holds—"Yes, sir," I mock, voice rough—fuck yeah—psycho fire simmers—Ed's laugh barks—"Cute," gruff and sharp—fuck—his hand flexes—keys jangle—fuck—my grin twists—"Big man's toy"—voice rough—king shit smirks—Ed steps—"Watch it"—fuck—psycho edge flares—he looms—stink thickens—coffee, sweat—fuck yeah—sexy clash burns—"See you, kid," gruff growl—fuck—my grin curls—"Count on it"—voice rough—fuck cuts deep.

Door clangs—Ed fades—boots echo—fuck—cell hums—bars bite—my grin holds—"King's game," I mutter—fuck yeah—psycho fire burns—Willa's frame glows—Clayton's blank stabs—Kayla's ghost hums—fuck—Ed's big—gruff—sexy foe—king shit sizes him—psycho edge twists—fuck roars loud.

Cell bites—bars hum—stink claws—fuck—my grin curls—"King's cage," I growl, voice rough—scratches scar—"E-K-A" glows—fuck yeah—psycho fire simmers—Willa's frame twists—Clayton's blank stabs—Kayla's ghost hums—fuck—door clangs—boots thunder—Ed looms—big fucker, meat slab—gray uniform strains—eyes black—"Up, kid," gruff growl cuts—fuck—my grin twists—"Hey, big man"—voice rough and sharp—king shit leans—psycho edge flares—fuck cuts deep.

"Exercise—move," he snaps—hand yanks—cuffs snap—chains bite—fuck—my grin holds—"Field trip?"—voice rough—Ed snarls—"Smart ass"—fuck—boots thud—hall echoes—stink thickens—piss, sweat, him—fuck yeah—psycho hum burns—doors clang—air shifts—cold bites—courtyard looms—grim slab—concrete cracks—razor wire coils—fuck—my grin curls—"King's court"—voice rough—Ed shoves—"Walk"—gruff and low—fuck—chains clank—king shit strides—psycho edge hums—sexy clash glows.

Court's bleak—gray sprawl—hoop sags—net's frayed—fuck—walls tower—scars bleed—"Die Pigs"—"J-Man '24"—fuck yeah—air's sharp—sweat stinks—yells bounce—"Fuck you!"—"Fresh bitch!"—fuck—my grin twists—"Home turf"—voice rough—Ed uncuffs—chains drop—fuck—hands flex—"Hoop's yours—thirty," gruff growl—fuck—ball rolls—rubber stinks—king shit smirks—"Still free here"—voice cuts—psycho fire flares—fuck yeah owns it.

Ball grips—fingers dig—fuck—my grin curls—"Game on," I say, voice rough—dribble slams—concrete bites—fuck yeah—psycho edge hums—Ed looms—arms cross—eyes bore—"Move it, kid"—gruff and low—fuck—my grin holds—"Watch king"—voice rough—step—fake—shoot—ball arcs—rim clangs—fuck—miss—Ed's laugh barks—"Weak"—fuck—psycho fire twists—ball rolls—snag it—dribble hard—fuck yeah—king shit burns—shoot—swish—fuck—my grin twists—"Got it"—voice rough—hot defiance flares.

Sweat beads—bare feet slap—fuck—ball slams—dribble weaves—psycho edge hums—Ed's eyes glint—"Faster"—gruff growl—fuck—my grin curls—"Speed's king"—voice rough—fake left—spin—shoot—rim sings—fuck yeah—swish—king shit smirks—"Still free"—voice cuts—fuck—Ed shifts—"Cocky shit"—gruff and low—fuck—ball bounces—snag it—dribble hard—psycho fire burns—shoot—clang—fuck—miss—Ed's grin cracks—"Slow"—fuck—my grin twists—"Watch this"—voice rough—fuck yeah owns it.

Court echoes—yells fade—fuck—sweat stings—ball grips—dribble slams—psycho edge flares—Willa's frame glows—Clayton's blank stabs—Kayla's ghost hums—fuck—my grin holds—"King's here"—voice rough—step—fake—shoot—swish—fuck yeah—Ed's eyes bore—"Ten left"—gruff growl—fuck—ball rolls—snag it—dribble hard—psycho fire twists—shoot—rim clangs—fuck—miss—Ed's laugh barks—"Done?"—fuck—my grin curls—"Never"—voice rough—king shit burns—hot defiance roars.

Time ticks—sweat drips—fuck—ball slams—dribble weaves—fuck yeah—psycho edge hums—Ed steps—"Wrap it"—gruff and low—fuck—my grin twists—"One more"—voice rough—fake—spin—shoot—swish—fuck—king shit smirks—"Free here"—voice cuts—Ed's hand yanks—cuffs snap—chains bite—fuck—my grin holds—"Good game"—voice rough—psycho fire flares—Ed growls—"Back"—fuck—court fades—boots thud—hall echoes—fuck yeah—king shit strides—hot defiance burns—fuck cuts sharp.

Cell bites—bars hum—stink claws—fuck—my grin twists—"King's cage"—voice rough—scratches scar—"E-K-A"—fuck yeah—psycho fire flickers—Willa's frame chokes—Clayton's blank cuts—Kayla's ghost fades—fuck—door clangs—Ed looms—big fucker—tray slams—"Chow, kid"—gruff growl—fuck—my grin curls—"Pig slop?"—voice rough—king shit sneers—psycho edge frays—fuck cuts sharp.

Tray's grim—gray mush pools—slop's thick—stinks sour—fuck—spoon bends—plastic cracks—my grin twists—"Fit for pigs"—voice rough—fuck—mush clumps—grains swirl—gray slime—fuck yeah—psycho hum snarls—Ed's boots shift—"Eat or starve"—gruff and low—fuck—my grin holds—"King's feast"—voice cuts—scoop it—slop drips—smears lips—fuck—tastes dead—salt, rot—psycho edge burns—fuck yeah sneers.

Cell hums—bars bite—fuck—my grin curls—"Pig shit"—voice rough—tray slams—slop splats—fuck—bare feet pace—concrete grinds—psycho fire twists—Willa's frame glows—Clayton's blank stabs—fuck—fingers scratch—nails bite—"K"—slashes deep—fuck yeah—slop stinks—sour clings—king shit snarls—"Not me"—voice rough—psycho edge frays—fuck cuts wild.

Light flickers—stink thickens—fuck—my grin twists—"Jail's bitch"—voice rough—tray sits—gray hardens—fuck—spoon snaps—psycho fire burns—pace quickens—fuck yeah—king shit sneers—"Fit for pigs"—mutter slips—fuck—cell locks—slop festers—psycho edge cracks—fuck roars low.

Cell hums—bars bite—stink claws—fuck—my grin twists—"King's cage"—voice rough—scratches scar—"E-K-A"—fuck yeah—psycho fire flickers—Willa's frame chokes—Clayton's blank cuts—Kayla's ghost hums—fuck—dark pools—light's dead—bunk creaks—bare feet grip—fuck—my grin curls—"Night's mine"—voice rough—psycho edge simmers—fuck cuts wild—door clangs—boots thunder—Ed storms—big fucker—meat slab—eyes black—"Up, kid"—gruff growl rips—fuck—my grin twists—"Late date, big man?"—rough and sharp—king shit leans—psycho edge flares.

"Smart mouth—done," he snarls—fist flies—meat hook slams—jaw cracks—fuck—blood sprays—my grin holds—"That all?"—voice rough—fuck yeah—psycho fire burns—Ed's growl rumbles—fist swings—gut sinks—fuck—air blasts—ribs groan—fuck—my grin curls—"Weak"—voice cuts—blood drips—king shit smirks—Ed's eyes flare—"Fucking punk"—gruff and low—fuck—fist slams—cheek splits—fuck yeah—psycho edge twists—cell spins—fuck—my grin twists—"More"—voice rough—hot clash roars.

He yanks—shirt rips—fuck—fists rain—gut, jaw, ribs—fuck—blood pools—lips crack—fuck yeah—psycho fire flares—my grin holds—"Big man's soft"—voice rough—Ed snarls—"Why'd you do it?"—fist slams—nose crunches—fuck—blood floods—"Nothing's mine"—voice cuts—fuck—king shit burns—Ed's fist flexes—"Liar"—gruff growl—fuck—my grin curls—"Prove it"—rough and sharp—psycho edge hums—fist flies—eye swells—fuck yeah—hot brutal sings—fuck cuts deep.

Cell echoes—bars hum—fuck—Ed looms—fists pound—ribs snap—fuck—blood spits—my grin twists—"King shit takes it"—voice rough—fuck yeah—psycho fire burns—Ed's growl rips—"Break, kid"—gruff and low—fuck—fist slams—lip bursts—fuck—my grin holds—"Try harder"—voice cuts—blood streams—king shit smirks—Ed's eyes glint—"Fucking psycho"—fuck—psycho edge flares—fist swings—gut caves—fuck yeah—hot clash twists—fuck roars wild.

He shoves—bunk slams—fuck—fists rain—back cracks—fuck—blood smears—my grin curls—"That all, big man?"—voice rough—fuck—Ed snarls—"Why her?"—fist slams—jaw pops—fuck yeah—psycho fire simmers—"Saved her"—voice cuts—lie's gold—fuck—Ed's fist flexes—"Bullshit"—gruff growl—fuck—my grin twists—"Nightcap's weak"—rough and sharp—king shit burns—fist flies—teeth rattle—fuck—psycho edge hums—hot brutal flares—fuck yeah owns it.

Ed steps—boots thud—fuck—blood pools—my grin holds—"Fun night"—voice rough—psycho fire twists—Ed growls—"Sleep tight"—gruff and low—fuck—door clangs—dark swallows—fuck yeah—king shit sprawls—bunk bites—blood drips—fuck—my grin curls—"Still king"—mutter slips—psycho edge burns—ribs scream—fuck—hot clash lingers—fuck cuts sharp—Willa's frame glows—Clayton's blank stabs—Kayla's ghost hums—fuck yeah roars—blood's sexy—fuck reigns wild.

DOWNER

Cell bites hard—bars hum low—stink claws at me—fuck—my grin twists tight—"King's cage," I growl, voice rough—blood crusts from Ed's fists—fuck yeah flickers—ribs ache—Willa's frame chokes my skull—Clayton's blank cuts—Kayla's ghost hums—fuck—door clangs—guard looms—"Call, punk"—boots thud—my grin curls—"Mommy time?"—voice rough—king shit leans—cuffs snap—chains bite—fuck—hall echoes—screen room glows—psycho edge frays—fuck cuts wild.

Screen flickers—Mom's there—eyes red, tears streak—"Ethan," her voice cracks—fuck—my grin holds—"Hey, Ma," I say, voice rough—fuck yeah simmers—she sobs—"It's tough—hard without you"—fuck—lunch tray slams down—gray slop pools—stink sours—my grin twists—"Fit for pigs," I mutter—voice cuts—Mom's hands shake—"Kacey asks—David's mad"—teary whine—fuck yeah—psycho edge burns—"Tough's life—slop's worse"—voice rough—king shit sneers—screen blurs—fuck cuts sharp.

"Jail's hell—why'd you?"—she chokes out—fuck—my grin
curls—"Didn't—Willa's lie," I snap—voice rough—fuck—slop
clumps—spoon bends—psycho fire twists—"Saved her,"
I growl—lie's gold—Mom sobs—"I failed you"—tears
drip—fuck yeah—my grin holds—"King's fine—eat this"—voice
cuts—slop smears—gray rot—fuck—tastes dead—ribs scream—king
shit burns—"Hard's you—here's me"—voice rough—screen
hums—psycho edge frays—fuck cuts dark.

"Kacey cries—home's empty," she whispers—fuck—my grin
twists—"Tell her king's back soon"—voice rough—fuck
yeah—slop stinks—sour clings—psycho fire simmers—"Lunch
here—pig shit"—voice cuts—Mom's eyes glint—"Love you"—teary
crack—fuck—my grin curls—"Yeah"—voice rough—king shit
smirks—screen blanks—fuck—tray slams—slop splats—psycho edge
burns—family vibe darkens—fuck yeah cuts wild.

Cell looms—chains clank—fuck—my grin holds—"Tough's hers," I
mutter—slop festers—ribs throb—fuck—psycho fire flickers—king
shit reigns—fuck cuts short.

Cell bites—bars hum—stink claws—fuck—my grin twists—"King's
cage," I growl—tray slams—dinner's grim—gray slop pools—sour
stink—fuck—spoon bends—"Pig shit," I snap—voice rough—fuck
yeah—psycho fire flickers—ribs ache—scoop it—slop smears—tastes
rot—fuck—my grin curls—"Jail's feast"—voice rough—king shit
sneers—tray splats—fuck—bare feet pace—psycho edge frays—fuck
cuts sharp.

Bunk creaks—hand slips—fuck—Kayla's ghost hums—cherry vape—blood drips—my grin twists—"Hey, Kayz," I mut-

ter—cock stirs—fuck yeah—psycho fire burns—fist grips—stroke slams—hot and quick—fuck—sweat beads—ribs scream—king shit smirks—"Still mine"—voice cuts—jerk hard—fuck—cum hits—bunk stains—psycho edge flares—"King's free," mutter slips—fuck yeah—dirty grind sings—fuck roars wild.

Floor's cold—push-ups hit—fuck—arms flex—blood crusts—fuck yeah—my grin holds—"King's grit," I growl—ten—twenty—sweat stings—fuck—psycho fire twists—pace quickens—thirty—forty—fuck—my grin curls—"Still free"—voice rough—muscle bites—king shit burns—cell hums—hot sweat hums—fuck yeah cuts short.

Cell clangs—bars bite—stink hums—fuck—my grin twists—"King's den"—voice rough—mail slot snaps—card drops—white, smug—fuck—Maxine's scrawl—"I know, Ethan—what happened"—fuck yeah—psycho edge flares—my grin curls—"Rat bitch"—voice rough—pen glints—"I know you—Willa's right"—fuck—king shit smirks—"She's got nothing"—voice cuts—psycho fire burns—card rips—fuck—my grin holds—"Maxine's bluff"—voice rough—fuck yeah—hot tension hums—Willa's frame glows—Clayton's blank stabs—Kayla's ghost twists—fuck—my grin twists—"Prove it, cunt"—mutter slips—psycho edge cuts—card shreds—fuck—king shit sneers—"Nothing's mine"—voice rough—fuck yeah—sexy doubt seeds—fuck roars wild.

Cell hums—tray slams—slop's gray—sour rot—fuck—my grin curls—"Pig feast"—voice rough—spoon cracks—slop smears—tastes dead—fuck yeah—psycho fire flickers—"Jail's king"—voice cuts—tray splats—fuck—ribs throb—king shit sneers—fuck cuts quick.

Floor bites—push-ups slam—fuck—sweat drips—arms burn—fuck yeah—my grin twists—"King's grit"—voice rough—twenty—thirty—ribs scream—fuck—psycho edge burns—"Free here"—voice cuts—forty—fuck—king shit smirks—cell hums—hot sweat sings—fuck roars fast.

Door clangs—cuffs snap—Jess waits—sage wafts—soft eyes—"Ethan"—voice calm—fuck—my grin holds—"Hey, doc"—voice rough—fuck yeah—psycho hum simmers—chair scrapes—"Feel it, Ethan"—fuck—my grin curls—"Numb's better"—voice cuts—Jess tilts—"Woods?"—fuck—psycho edge twists—"Jayden's mess—saved her"—lie's gold—fuck yeah—her pen scratches—"Feel her?"—sage stings—fuck—my grin twists—"Nothing—king's cool"—voice rough—Jess nods—"Breathe"—fuck—inhale—exhale—bullshit hums—psycho fire burns—"Numb's king"—mutter slips—fuck yeah—king shit smirks—fuck cuts dark.

Cell clangs—bars bite—stink hums—fuck—my grin twists—"King's cage"—voice rough—blood crusts—Ed's fists scar—fuck yeah—psycho fire flickers—ribs throb—Willa's frame chokes—Clayton's blank cuts—Kayla's ghost hums—fuck—door slams—boots thud—Jacobs strides—suit crisp, eyes hard—Mia trails—hot as fuck—black skirt tight—blouse pops—dark hair spills—red lips glint—fuck—my grin curls—"Hey, gorgeous"—voice rough—king shit leers—psycho edge flares—fuck cuts wild.

"Sit, Ethan"—Jacobs snaps—tablet glows—fuck—cuffs clank—my grin holds—"What's cooking?"—voice rough—fuck yeah—Mia's pen scratches—legs cross—skirt rides—fuck—psycho hum burns—Jacobs leans—"Social media's wild—Maxine's hinting—Willa's witness now"—fuck—my grin twists—"Rat bitch—witch bitch"—voice cuts—king shit smirks—Mia's eyes glint—"Maxine's card—'I know'—she's smug"—fuck—psycho edge twists—"She's got jack"—voice rough—fuck yeah—Jacobs slides—"Willa's state—swears you stabbed—Jayden's the bad guy"—fuck—my grin curls—"Jayden's dead—hero shit"—voice cuts—sexy legal twist hums.

"Evidence stacks—Willa's tight—Clayton's blank—Maxine's noise," Jacobs growls—tablet hums—fuck—my grin holds—"Willa's lying—Jayden's psycho—saved her"—voice rough—fuck yeah—psycho fire burns—Mia leans—"Social media's fire—memorial posts—'Justice for Kayla'—Maxine's stoking"—fuck—my grin twists—"Maxine's a cunt—nothing's real"—voice cuts—king shit sneers—Jacobs taps—"Willa's deal—state witness—pins you—Jayden's enemy"—fuck—psycho edge flares—"Jayden's my kill—Willa's twist"—voice rough—fuck yeah—court case sparks—fuck cuts deep.

"Case status—trial looms—Halloween," Jacobs says—eyes bore—fuck—my grin curls—"Witchy bitch—perfect"—voice rough—fuck yeah—Mia's pen scratches—"Maxine's posts—'He's guilty'—memorial's hot"—fuck—psycho fire twists—"She's bluffing—Jayden's blood's mine"—voice cuts—king shit burns—Jacobs leans—"Evidence—knife's yours—Willa's sworn—Clayton's void"—fuck—my grin holds—"Jayden's blade—saved her—Willa's hex"—voice rough—fuck yeah—sexy clash hums—Mia's eyes glint—"Social's wild—fans, haters—Maxine's loud"—fuck—psycho edge burns—fuck cuts wild.

"Appeal's thin—Willa's strong—Jayden's dead," Jacobs snaps—tablet dims—fuck—my grin twists—"King shit fights—Willa's fucked"—voice rough—fuck yeah—psycho fire flares—Mia leans—"Memorial's viral—'Kayla's angel'—Maxine's threat"—fuck—my grin curls—"Nothing's hers—Jayden's mine"—voice cuts—king shit smirks—Jacobs stands—"Court's fire—Willa's move"—fuck—psycho edge twists—"Halloween's mine"—voice rough—fuck yeah—sexy legal twist burns—cuffs clank—Ed yanks—"Back"—fuck—my grin holds—"King's game"—mutter slips—fuck cuts deep—court case roars—fuck yeah reigns.

[Patsy Franklin]

this is horrible, how can someone have such an evil soul

[Jake Allen]

Life without parole at the least and don't forget the parents who failed to raise a human being.

[Lorraine Moore]

I read he was expelled for beating a teacher up

[Farahsunkiss]

@stacipearse he looks so much like that guy you hooked up with a few weeks back?

[Marcus Parson]

I bet he used to kill the family pets. That's the first sign of a psychopath

[K. Taboo]

Ethan bae

Free Falling

Cell hums low—bars bite—stink claws—fuck—my grin twists tight—"King's cage," I growl—voice rough—blood crusts—slop festers—fuck yeah roars—ribs throb—Willa's frame chokes—Clayton's blank fades—Kayla's ghost hums—fuck—my grin curls—"Ed's throat—mine"—voice rough—psycho edge burns—toothbrush snaps in my grip—handle gleams—fuck—fingers grip hard—king shit smirks—"Big man's done," mutter slips—fuck yeah—sexy menace flares—fighter vibe amps—fuck cuts wild.

Dark pools—bars hum—fuck—my grin holds—"Ed's neck—slit slow," I mutter—voice rough—fuck yeah—psycho fire twists—toothbrush cracks—plastic bends—fuck—fingers scrape—edge sharpens—cell's cold—my grin curls—"Big fucker bleeds"—voice cuts—fuck—rub hard—handle bites—psycho edge hums—"Throat's soft—easy"—mutter slips—fuck yeah—king shit grins—sharpening sings—fuck roars dark.

Concrete grinds—fingers bleed—fuck—my grin twists—"Ed's eyes—wide, dead"—voice rough—fuck—psycho fire burns—toothbrush gleams—blade's born—fuck yeah—ribs scream—"Big man's meat—mine"—voice cuts—fuck—sharpen fast—edge cuts—king shit smirks—"Choke on it"—mutter slips—fuck—psycho edge flares—sexy menace hums—fighter vibe twists—fuck yeah—cell's tight—fuck cuts sharp.

Light flickers—stink thickens—fuck—my grin curls—"Ed's blood—hot spill"—voice rough—fuck yeah—psycho fire roars—handle's keen—thumb tests—fuck—skin splits—blood beads—my grin holds—"Perfect—his end"—voice cuts—fuck—king shit sneers—sharpening hums—Willa's frame glows—Kayla's ghost hums—fuck—my grin twists—"Big man's fucked"—mutter slips—psycho edge burns—fighter vibe amps—fuck yeah—dark grin shines—fuck roars wild.

Cell spins—bars fade—fuck—my grin curls—"Ed's throat—slash deep"—voice rough—fuck—psycho fire twists—toothbrush blade gleams—fingers grip—fuck yeah—ribs throb—"Big fucker drops—slow"—voice cuts—fuck—sharpen hard—edge bites—king shit smirks—"King's kill"—mutter slips—fuck—psycho edge hums—sexy menace flares—fighter vibe burns—fuck yeah—cell's cold—fuck cuts deep—Ed's end looms—fuck roars free.

Cell hums—bars bite—stink claws—fuck—my grin twists—"King's cage"—voice rough—toothbrush blade hides—fuck yeah—psycho fire simmers—ribs throb—Willa's frame chokes—Kayla's ghost hums—fuck—door clangs—boots thud—Ed looms—big fucker—meat slab—gray tray drops—"Draw, kid"—gruff

growl—fuck—my grin curls—"Art time, big man?"—voice
rough—king shit sneers—psycho edge flares—fuck cuts wild.

Tray's sparse—paper curls—safety pencil rolls—fuck—blunt
tip—rubber grip—joke's thick—my grin twists—"Safety
shit?"—voice rough—fuck yeah—psycho fire burns—Ed's
eyes glint—"Keep you busy"—gruff and low—fuck—my
grin holds—"Busy's king"—voice cuts—fingers snatch—pencil
grips—fuck—king shit smirks—ironic twist hums—psycho edge
twists—fuck yeah—tension builds—fuck roars hot.

Paper's rough—pencil drags—fuck—my grin curls—"Kayla's
blood—red lines"—voice rough—fuck—psycho fire flares—tip
scratches—blunt bites—fuck yeah—her eyes sketch—wide,
dead—blood pools—fuck—my grin twists—"Safety's a
laugh"—voice cuts—king shit sneers—Kayla's throat—slash
marks—pencil grinds—fuck—psycho edge hums—"Ed's joke—dull
blade"—mutter slips—fuck yeah—twisted humor sings—fuck cuts
sharp.

Cell's cold—stink thickens—fuck—my grin holds—"Her
lips—cherry red"—voice rough—fuck—pencil drags—blunt
smears—psycho fire burns—Kayla's chest—stab scars—fuck
yeah—my grin curls—"Safety's weak—blood's hot"—voice
cuts—fuck—king shit smirks—paper tears—pencil
fights—fuck—psycho edge flares—ironic heat twists—fuck
yeah—tension hums—fuck roars wild.

Ed looms—boots thud—fuck—my grin twists—"Look, big
man"—voice rough—fuck—psycho fire simmers—paper lifts—Kayla bleeds—pencil's dull—fuck yeah—his eyes glint—"Fucked

up, kid"—gruff growl—fuck—my grin holds—"King's art"—voice cuts—fuck—psycho edge burns—"Safety's irony—her blood"—mutter slips—fuck yeah—twisted humor flares—tension builds—fuck cuts deep—sketch glows—fuck roars hot.

Cell hums—bars bite—stink claws—fuck—my grin twists—"King's cage"—voice rough—Kayla's sketch bleeds—fuck yeah—psycho fire simmers—ribs throb—door clangs—Ed looms—"Out, kid"—gruff growl—fuck—my grin curls—"Playtime, big man?"—voice rough—cuffs snap—chains bite—fuck—boots thud—hall echoes—courtyard looms—gray sprawl—razor wire glints—fuck—my grin holds—"King's turf"—voice cuts—psycho edge flares—fuck yeah—hot shift hums.

Ed uncuffs—chains drop—fuck—air bites—sweat stinks—yells bounce—"Fresh meat!"—fuck—my grin twists—"Bring it"—voice rough—fuck yeah—psycho fire burns—court's grim—concrete cracks—hoop sags—fuck—steps thud—gang rolls—four fuckers—white ink—swastikas crawl—skinny one sneers—"Pretty boy"—fists flex—fuck—my grin curls—"That all, fuckers?"—voice rough—king shit smirks—fighter vibe amps—fuck yeah—bloody clash sparks.

Lead lunges—fist flies—swastika blurs—fuck—jaw cracks—blood sprays—my grin holds—"Weak shit"—voice cuts—fuck—psycho edge roars—fist slams—nose crunches—fuck yeah—he staggers—red spills—"Fucking punk!"—skinny shrieks—fuck—my grin twists—"King hits"—voice rough—two rush—fists swing—ribs scream—fuck—duck—jab—gut caves—fuck yeah—psycho fire flares—king shit fights—fuck cuts wild.

Third jumps—swastika gleams—fist slams—eye swells—fuck—my grin curls—"More"—voice rough—fuck—kick flies—knee cracks—fuck yeah—he drops—groans—psycho edge burns—lead's back—fist swings—lip bursts—fuck—my grin holds—"That all, fuckers?"—voice cuts—fuck—king shit smirks—jab—jaw pops—fuck yeah—bloody grin twists—fighter vibe roars—fuck cuts hot.

Skinny grabs—arms lock—fuck—my grin twists—"Pussy grip"—voice rough—psycho fire flares—head snaps—skull cracks—fuck—he reels—"Nazi bitch!"—fuck yeah—fourth lunges—fist flies—gut sinks—fuck—my grin curls—"King's up"—voice cuts—fuck—elbow slams—nose bleeds—psycho edge hums—lead swings—ribs snap—fuck—my grin holds—"Fucking weak"—voice rough—fuck yeah—king shit fights—fuck roars wild.

Gang staggers—blood pools—fuck—my grin twists—"Done, fuckers?"—voice rough—psycho fire burns—skinny spits—"Dead meat"—fuck—my grin curls—"Try it"—voice cuts—fuck yeah—fighter vibe flares—Ed looms—"Enough!"—gruff growl—fuck—boots thud—cuffs snap—chains bite—fuck—my grin holds—"King's game"—voice rough—psycho edge hums—court bleeds—fuck yeah—hot clash fades—fuck cuts deep.

[Crash burn]

you deserve to go to the coldest, darkest prison cell they have with some 6.4 dude that's gonna call you fluffy cheeks for the next 60 years or so

[Megan McNeil]

Why were these kids out so late? I would never let my daughter stay out after 10pm.

[Jasper Peters]

if I was this murderer's mother I would ask that they give my son the death sentence

[Macerieh]

fuck you! You spawn of Satan

[Xx_ariah]

ur hot but please die

[SarahDuckitt]

god will have his revenge. The lord will have no mercy on your soul. May you be banished to the fires of hell for one thousand years. Jesus will make sure of this.

[Brycesratton]

if you ever get out, I am gonna kidnap and torture you boy

[K. Taboo]

Ethan, Marry me

THE SPIRAL

C ell hums—bars bite—stink claws—fuck
  My grin twists—"King's cage"—voice rough
Blood crusts—gang's red stains—fuck yeah
Psycho fire—roars—ribs scream

Toothbrushshank—hides—Willa's frame—chokes
Kayla's ghost—hums—fuck—door slams
Boots thunder—Ed storms—big fucker—meat slab
Eyes blaze—"Toothbrush shank, kid?"—gruff growl rips

Fuck—my grin curls—"Whatshank, big man?"—voice rough
King shit—sneers—psycho edge—flares—fuck cuts—wild
"Found it—your blade"—he snarls—hand yanks
Tray crashes—fuck—toothbrush gleams—sharp tip glints

My grin twists—"Safety'sgone"—voice rough
Fuck yeah—psycho fire—burns—Ed's fist—flexes
Meat hooks—fuck—"Planning me?"—gruff—low
Fuck—my grin holds—"Dream on"—voice cuts

Fuck—Ed's slap—flies—palmcracks—face burns
Fuck—blood spits—my grin curls—"Hit—again—fucker"—voice
rough
Psycho edge—roars—sexy clash—steams
Fuck yeah—amps—fuck cuts—wild

He grabs—shirt rips—fuck—slapslams
Cheek   splits—fuck—blood   sprays—my   grin
twists—"That—all?"—voice cuts
Fuck—psycho   fire—flares—Ed's   growl—"Fucking   psy-
cho"—gruff—sharp
Fuck—slap flies—jaw pops—fuck yeah

My grin holds—"More"—voicerough
King shit—spits—red drips—Ed's eyes—flare—"Shank's—mine"
Fuck—my grin curls—"Prove—it"—voice cuts
Fuck—psycho edge—burns—slap cracks—lip bursts

Fuck—sexy fighter—hums—fuckyeah—roars
Cell spins—bars blur—fuck—Ed looms
Slap slams—eye swells—fuck—my grin twists—"Big man—soft"—voice rough
Psycho fire—twists—Ed snarls—"Why—me?"—gruff—growl

Fuck—my grinholds—"King's—game"—voice cuts
Fuck yeah—slap flies—nose crunches—blood floods
Fuck—psycho edge—flares—"Hit—again—fucker"—voice rough
King shit—grins—Ed's fist—"Fucking—nut"—fuck

Slap slams—teeth rattle—fuckyeah
Hot clash—steams—fuck cuts—wild
He shoves—wall bites—fuck—slap cracks
Ribs groan—fuck—blood pools—my grin curls—"Weak—shit"—voice rough

Psycho fire—burns—Ed'sgrowl—"Shank's—you"—gruff—low
Fuck—my grin twists—"Nothing's—mine"—voice cuts
Fuck—king shit—spits—slap flies—face burns
Fuck yeah—psycho edge—roars—"More—fucker"—voice rough

Ed'seyes—"Break—soon"—fuck—my grin holds—"Try—harder"—voice cuts
Fuck—sexy fighter—flares—fuck yeah—tension—steams

Fuck roars—wild
Ed steps—boots thud—fuck—blood drips

My grintwists—"King's—still—up"—voice rough
Psycho fire—simmers—Ed growls—"Next—time"—gruff—sharp
Fuck—door clangs—dark swallows—fuck yeah
King shit—sprawls—cell hums—blood stains—fuck

My grincurls—"Hit—again"—mutter slips
Psycho edge—burns—fighter vibe—amps
Fuck cuts—deep—spiral twists—fuck roars—free
Cell hums—bars bite—stink claws—fuck

My grintwists—"King's—cage"—voice rough
Blood crusts—shank's gone—fuck yeah
Psycho fire—simmers—ribs scream—Ed's slaps—scar
Willa's frame—chokes—Kayla's ghost—hums—fuck

Mail slot—clangs—lettersspill—white chaos—fuck
My grin curls—"Fan—mail—fuckers"—voice rough
King shit—sneers—psycho edge—flares—fuck cuts—wild
First's red—"You're—monster"—scrawl bites—fuck

My grintwists—"Damn—right"—voice rough
Fuck yeah—psycho fire—burns—"Sick—fuck—rot"—ink bleeds
Fuck—my grin holds "They're—obsessed"—voice cuts
King shit—smirks—hater's rage—hums—fuck

Fingersrip—paper—shreds—psycho edge—twists
"Love—me"—mutter slips—fuck yeah—hot chaos—amps
Fuck roars—wild
Next's pink—"Marry—me"—loops curl—fuck

My grincurls—"Crazy—bitch"—voice rough
Fuck—"You're—hot—killer king"—pen glints—fuck yeah
Psycho fire—flares—"Fuck—me—in blood"—fuck
My grin twists—"Fans—drool"—voice cuts

King shit—sneers—egoswells—fuck—letter creases
Psycho edge—hums—"They—want—it"—mutter slips
Fuck yeah—sexy mess—burns—fuck cuts—sharp
Last's blue—"Praying—for—you"—old lady—shakes—fuck

My grinholds—"Sweet—granny"—voice rough
Fuck—"God—save—soul"—ink quivers—fuck yeah
Psycho fire—simmers—"Too—late"—voice cuts
Fuck—my grin curls—"They're—hooked"—voice rough

King shit—smirks—prayershum—fuck—paper folds
Psycho edge—twists—"Love—pity"—mutter slips
Fuck yeah—hot chaos—builds—fuck roars—deep
Cell spins—letters pile—fuck—my grin twists—"Haters—fans—old
bags"—voice rough

Fuck—psychofire—burns—"Monster—marry—pray"—fuck yeah
King shit—sneers—"They're—obsessed"—voice cuts
Fuck—ribs ache—ego flares—psycho edge—hums
"King's—star"—mutter slips—fuck—letters glow

Hot mess—amps—fuckyeah—spiral—twists
Fuck cuts—wild
Cell hums—bars bite—stink claws—fuck
My grin twists—"King's—cage"—voice rough

Blood crusts—letterspile—fuck yeah
Psycho fire—simmers—ribs scream—Ed's slaps—scar
Willa's frame—chokes—Kayla's ghost—hums—fuck
Mail slot—clangs—envelope drops—white venom

Maxine's scrawl—fuck—my grincurls—"Rat—bitch"—voice rough
King shit—sneers—psycho edge—flares—fuck cuts—wild

Tear it—paper rips—pic spills—Willa—Clayton—fuck
Arms   locked—smiles   glint—dating—Maxine's
note—"They're—fucking—Ethan—bro—witch"

Fuck—my grintwists—"Betrayed—by—bitches"—voice rough
Fuck yeah—psycho fire—roars—pic's hot—Willa's red
Clay's cap—fuck—fingers clutch—rage hums
Maxine's   smug—"Knew—you'd—burn"—fuck—my   grin
curls—"She's—dead"—voice cuts

King shit—snarls—sexyrage—twists—fuck yeah
Knife—twists—deep
Eyes   burn—pic   glares—fuck—my   grin
holds—"Willa's—cunt—Clay's—bitch"—voice rough
Fuck—psycho   edge—flares—Maxine's
ink—"They're—tight—your—fault"

Fuck yeah—fingers rip—picshreds—fuck
Wall   cracks—fist   slams—blood   smears—my   grin
twists—"I'll—gut—'em"—voice cuts
Fuck—ribs scream—psycho fire—burns—Willa's frame—chokes
Clayton's   blank—betrays—fuck—my   grin   curls—"Fuck-
ing—mine"—voice rough

King shit—roars—fighter'sfury—flares—fuck yeah
Unhinged—heat—hums—fuck cuts—wild
Cell   spins—bars   blur—fuck—my   grin
twists—"Clay's—throat—Willa's—eyes"—voicerough
Fuck—psycho fire—twists—shreds fly—Maxine's laugh

Fuck yeah—fist slams—wallbleeds—fuck
My grin holds—"Betrayed—gut—'em"—voice cuts
Fuck—king shit—sneers—"They're—dead"—mutter slips
Psycho edge—burns—sexy rage—steams—fuck

Fist cracks—knucklessplit—fuck yeah
Fighter vibe—amps—fuck cuts—wild
Paper   dust—blood   drips—fuck—my   grin   curls—"Max-
ine's—next"—voice rough
Fuck—psycho fire—roars—Willa's smile—Clay's grin

Fuck yeah—my grintwists—"I'll—carve—'em"—voice cuts
Fuck—king shit—snarls—cell hums—rage twists
Fuck—psycho edge—flares—"Bitches—burn"—mutter slips
Fuck yeah—hot fury—sings—fuck roars—deep

Knife twists—fuck cuts—wild
Cell hums—bars bite—stink claws—fuck

My grin twists—"King's—cage"—voice rough
Blood crusts—wall bleeds—fuck yeah

Psycho fire—roars—ribsscream—Willa's frame—chokes
Clayton's pic—rips—Maxine's laugh—hums—fuck
Door   clangs—boots   thud—guard   looms—"Thera-
pist—punk"—fuck
My grin curls—"Jess—time"—voice rough

Cuffs snap—chainsbite—fuck—hall echoes
Screen room—glows—psycho edge—flares—fuck cuts—wild
Jess   waits—sage   wafts—soft   eyes—brown
hair—loose—"Ethan"—voice calm
Fuck—my grin twists—"Hey—doc"—voice rough

Fuck yeah—psychofire—simmers—chair scrapes
Cuffs   clank—my   grin   holds—"Willa—Clay—fucking—be-
trayed—me"—voice cuts
Fuck—Jess tilts—"Betrayed—how?"—sage stings
Fuck—my   grin   curls—"Maxine's—pic—they're—tight—fuck-
ing—bitches"—voice rough

Psycho edge—burns—fuckyeah—sexy unravel—hums
Tension—amps—fuck roars—wild
"Willa—Clayton?"—Jess probes—pen hovers—fuck

My grin twists—"Yeah—my—witch—my—bro—fucking"—voice
rough

Fuck — p s y c h o fi r e — fl a r e s — " S h e ' s — f r a m -
ing—Clay's—blank—now—this"
Fuck yeah—Jess leans—"Feel—that?"—fuck
My grin curls—"Rage—hot"—voice cuts
Fuck—king shit—snarls—"They're—dead"—mutter slips

Psycho edge—twists—sagehums—fuck yeah
Tension—steams—fuck cuts—sharp
"Breathe—Ethan"—Jess says—hands lift—fuck
My grin holds—"Bull—shit"—voice rough—fuck

I n h a l e — h o l d — e x h a l e — p s y -
chofire—burns—"Willa's—cunt—Clay's—bitch"—voice cuts
Fuck yeah—Jess scribbles—"Why'd—they?"—fuck
My   grin
twists—"Fuck—me—over—Willa's—hex—Clay's—weak"—voice
rough
Fuck—psycho edge—flares—"Knife's—ready"—mutter slips

Fuck yeah—sexychaos—hums—Jess—"Knife?"—fuck
Tension—amps—fuck roars—wild
"Yeah—knife"—my   grin

curls—"Ed's—throat—Willa's—eyes—Clay's—gut"—voice rough
Fuck—psycho fire—roars—Jess's eyes—glint—"Here?"—fuck

My grintwists—"I'd—blow—this—shithole—up"—voice cuts
Fuck yeah—king shit—sneers—"Boom—fuckers—gone"—fuck
Jess leans—"Blow—how?"—sage stings—fuck
My grin holds—"Shank—fire—what—ever"—voice rough

Psychoedge—burns—"They're—mine"—mutter slips
Fuck yeah—sexy unravel—twists—fuck cuts—deep
"Feel—them?"—Jess probes—pen scratches—fuck
My grin curls—"Betray—hot—red"—voice rough

F   u   c   k   —   p   s   y   -
chofire—flares—"Willa's—laugh—Clay's—blank—fuck—ing"
Fuck yeah—Jess tilts—"Kill—them?"—fuck
My grin twists—"Yeah—gut—'em—blow—it"—voice cuts
Fuck—king shit—smirks—"Shithole's—dust"—fuck

Psychoedge—hums—"Knife's—king"—mutter slips
Fuck yeah—tension—steams—Jess—"Why—blow—it?"—fuck
My grin holds—"Free—me—fuckers—burn"—voice rough
Fuck—sexy chaos—roars—fuck cuts—wild

"Breathe—again"—Jesssays—hands rise—fuck
My grin twists—"Fuck—that"—voice rough
Psycho   fire—burns—"Willa's—hex—Clay's—dick—Max-
ine's—smug"—fuck yeah
Jess—"Feel—here?"—fuck—my   grin
curls—"Rage—king's—rage"—voice cuts

Fuck—psychoedge—flares—"I'd—blow—it—shank—'em"—fuck
Jess—"Shank—who?"—sage hums—fuck
My grin twists—"Ed—Willa—Clay—fuck—ers"—voice rough
Fuck yeah—king shit—snarls—"Shithole's—mine"—mutter slips

Fuck—tension—amps—fuckroars—wild
"Feel—you?"—Jess probes—eyes lock—fuck
My grin holds—"King—wild"—voice rough
Fuck—psycho fire—roars—"Betray—blow—it"—fuck yeah

J e s s — " W i l d — h o w ? " — f u c k — m y
grincurls—"Shank—boom—free"—voice cuts
F   u   c   k   —   k   i   n   g
shit—sneers—"They're—obsessed—burn—'em"—fuck
Psycho edge—twists—"I'd—blow—this—shit—hole—up"—voice
rough
Fuck yeah—sexy unravel—steams—Jess—"Feel—that?"—fuck

My grintwists—"Yeah—hot"—voice cuts
Fuck—tension—burns—fuck roars—wild
Shit—hole's—dust—fuck yeah—reigns
Cell hums—bars bite—stink claws—fuck

My grintwists—"King's—cage"—voice rough
Blood crusts—wall bleeds—fuck yeah
Psycho fire—roars—ribs scream—Willa's frame—chokes
Clayton's pic—rips—Maxine's laugh—hums—fuck

Door clangs—boots thud—guardlooms—"Visit—punk"—fuck
My grin curls—"Mom—my's—here"—voice rough
Cuffs snap—chains bite—fuck—hall echoes
Screen room—glows—psycho edge—flares—fuck cuts—wild

Mom's   there—screenflickers—eyes   red—tears
streak—"Ethan"—voice cracks
Fuck—my grin twists—"Hey—Ma"—voice rough
Fuck yeah—psycho fire—simmers—chains clank
Her hands—shake—"I—failed—you"—teary whine—fuck

My grincurls—"You—never—loved—me!"—voice cuts
Fuck—ribs   burn—psycho
edge—roars—"Fuck—ing—failed—drunk—bitch"

Fuck yeah—Mom sobs—"I—tried"—fuck
My grin twists—"Bull—shit!"—voice rough

King shit—snarls—sexyrage—flares—fuck cuts—sharp
"David's—mad—Kacey—cries"—she chokes—fuck
My grin holds—"Never—loved—me—fuck—'em"—voice cuts
Fuck—psycho fire—twists—"You—let—him—hit—me"—fuck
yeah

Mom'seyes—glint—"I—was—scared"—teary crack—fuck
My grin curls—"Weak—cunt"—voice rough
Fuck—chains   bite—psycho
edge—burns—"Failed—me—fuck—you"—voice cuts
Fuck yeah—king shit—screams—"Never—cared!"—fuck

Mom—"I—love—you"—fuck—my grintwists—"Liar!"—voice
rough
Sexy chaos—hums—fuck roars—wild
Screen   blurs—tears   flood—fuck—my   grin
holds—"You—fucked—me—left—me"—voice cuts
Fuck—psycho fire—flares—"Drunk—slut—David's—bitch"—fuck
yeah

M o m — " I — t r i e d — E t h a n " — f u c k — m y g r i n
curls—"Fuck—your—try!"—voice rough

Fuck—chains snap—fist slams—screen cracks—fuck yeah
Psycho edge—roars—"Never—loved—me—fuck—you!"—voice
cuts
Fuck—king shit—kicks—wall shakes—fuck—sexy unravel—twists

Fuck cuts—deep
"Ethan—stop!"—she   screams—fuck—my   grin
twists—"Fuck—you—all!"—voice rough
Psycho fire—burns—chains yank—fist flies—screen bleeds—fuck
yeah
My   grin   holds—"You're—nothing!"—voice
cuts—fuck—Mom—"My—baby"—fuck

My grincurls—"Fuck—your—baby!"—voice rough
Fuck—psycho edge—flares—kick slams—screen splits
Fuck yeah—king shit—screams—"Betray—fuck—you!"—fuck
Sexy rage—steams—fuck roars—wild

Door slams—Ed storms—bigfucker—"Down—kid!"—gruff growl
Fuck—my grin twists—"Fuck—you—big—man!"—voice rough
Psycho fire—roars—chains bite—Ed grabs—meat hooks—fuck
My grin holds—"Hit—me—fucker!"—voice cuts—fuck

Kick flies—Ed's gut—fuckyeah—psycho edge—burns
Ed   yanks—arms   lock—fuck—my   grin

curls—"Fuck—you—all!"—voice rough
King shit—kicks—bloody grin—flares—fuck—sexy chaos—twists
Fuck cuts—wild

Ed   hauls—chains   drag—fuck—mygrin
twists—"You're—dead!"—voice rough
Psycho fire—flares—legs kick—screen fades—fuck yeah
Mom—"Ethan!"—fuck—my   grin
holds—"Fuck—your—tears!"—voice cuts
Fuck—Ed   slams—wall   cracks—fuck—my   grin
curls—"More—fucker!"—voice rough

P   s   y   c   h   o
edge—roars—bloodygrin—shines—"Fuck—you—all!"—voice cuts
Fuck yeah—king shit—screams—hall echoes—fuck
Sexy fighter—steams—fuck roars—wild
Cell   looms—Ed   shoves—fuck—my   grin
twists—"King's—still—up"—voice rough

Psycho fire—burns—chainssnap—floor bites—fuck yeah
Bloody grin—holds—"Fuck—you—all!"—mutter slips—fuck
Ed—"Fucking—nut"—gruff—low—fuck—door   clangs—dark
swallows
Psycho edge—flares—sexy unravel—twists—fuck

King shit—reigns—fuckcuts—deep—spiral—screams
Fuck yeah—roars

[BruceFenter]

This kid needs some discipline when he was younger. I would have beaten some sense into him.

[AlanPatall]

My dad used the belt on me and I turned out fine. Problem here is, this boy never got a good hiding and now he does this.

[TonyDerwebt]

spank the child and you create a decent adult

[PatrickNobu]

I hope they beat him up every day in prison

[K. Taboo]

Ethan, I want to have your children

[Dreamcatcher5432]

you gonna get ripped to shreds in prison

[Deeteryumy]

DIE MOTHERFUCKER

[Suzie24fsd]

I love you Ethan

[Reefer653]

@Suzie24fsd are you dumb or something

[PatsyPallet]

sucks that he is too young for the death penalty

FRIGHT NIGHT

Cell hums—bars bite—stink claws—fuck
My grin twists—"King's cage"—voice rough
Blood crusts—Mom's "I failed" echoes—fuck yeah
Psycho fire—flickers—ribs scream

Dark pools—bunk creaks—fuck
Eyes shut—Kayla's ghost—glows
Blood drips—cherry hums—fuck
My grin curls—"Fuck off!"—voice rough

Psycho edge—twists—nightmarebites
Fuck cuts—wild
Sleep hits—dark floods—fuck
Kayla's eyes—wide, dead—blood pours

Throat slashes—fuck
My grin twists—"No!"—voice cracks
Fuck yeah—psycho fire—roars
Her "Why?"—gurgles—fuck

Hands claw—sheets rip—fuck
Body thrashes—bunk shakes
Kayla's blood—hot, red—fuck
My grin curls—"Fuck off!"—voice rough

Psycho edge—burns—nightmarespins
Fuck roars—wild
Wall looms—head slams—fuck
Crack echoes—blood smears—fuck yeah

My grin twists—"Getout!"—voice cuts
Fuck—Kayla's ghost—cherry fades
Stab scars—glow—psycho fire—flares
Head slams—wall bites—fuck

Ribs scream—"Fuck off!"—voicerough
Fuck—bunk creaks—thrash hard

Psycho edge—twists—dark terror—hums
Fuck yeah—sexy chaos—burns

Fuck cuts—deep
Lights flash—door clangs—fuck
Ed storms—big fucker—"Down, kid!"—gruff growl
Fuck—my grin curls—"Fuck you!"—voice rough

Head slams—blood drips—fuckyeah
Psycho fire—roars—Kayla's ghost—blood pools
Fuck—Ed grabs—meat hooks
Fuck—my grin twists—"Fuck off!"—voice cuts

Fuck—head slams—wall cracks
Psycho edge—flares—sexy terror—twists
Fuck yeah—vibes scream
Fuck roars—wild

Guards rush—hands yank—fuck
My grin holds—"Kayla—fuck!"—voice rough
Psycho fire—burns—thrash hard
Chains bite—fuck yeah

Ed snarls—"Meds!"—fuck
Pill's white—hand slams—mouth twists
Fuck—my grin curls—"Fuck you all!"—voice cuts
Fuck—head slams—blood sprays

Psycho edge—roars—guardspin—fuck
Pill forced—throat burns—fuck yeah
Sexy chaos—hums
Fuck cuts—deep

Dark spins—Kayla fades—fuck
My grin twists—"No!"—voice rough
Psycho fire—flickers—head slams
Wall bleeds—fuck

Ed growls—"Swallow,fucker"—gruff and low
Fuck—my grin holds—"Fuck off!"—voice cuts
Fuck yeah—pill slides—bitter sting
Psycho edge—twists—body slumps—fuck

Kayla's ghost—blood dims
Fuck—my grin curls—"King's down"—mutter slips
Dark terror—burns—fuck yeah
Vibes hum—fuck fades—wild

Cell hums—bars blur—fuck
My grin twists—"Fuck..."—voice rough
Psycho fire—dims—meds sink
Dark swallows—fuck yeah

Nightmare fades—bloodygrin—lingers
Fuck cuts—slow
Cell hums—bars bite—stink claws—fuck
My grin twists—"King's cage"—voice rough

Blood crusts—nightmaremeds—fade
Fuck yeah—psycho fire—roars
Ribs scream—Willa's frame—chokes
Clayton's pic—burns—fuck

Door clangs—boots thud
Ed looms—"Call, kid"—gruff growl
Fuck—my grin curls—"Judge time, big man?"—voice rough
Cuffs snap—chains bite—fuck

Hall echoes—screen room—glows
Psycho edge—flares—fuck cuts—wild

Room's stark—screen hums—table gleams—fuck
Ed shoves—"Sit"—gruff and low

Fuck—my grin twists—"King'sthrone"—voice rough
Fuck yeah—chains clank—screen flickers
Judge pops—face pinched—"Ethan, present"—voice drones
Fuck—my grin curls—"Yeah, fucker"—voice cuts

Psycho fire—burns—Edgrowls—"Watch it"
Fuck—my grin holds—"They're all liars!"—voice rough
Fuck yeah—sexy meltdown—hums
Vibes twist—fuck roars—wild

"Trial update"—judgesnaps—eyes bore
Fuck—my grin twists—"Willa's lies—Clay's blank!"—voice cuts
Fuck—psycho edge—flares—"Maxine's smug—fuck 'em!"
Fuck yeah—judge frowns—"Order!"—fuck

My grin curls—"Fuck yourorder!"—voice rough
Fist bangs—table shakes—fuck
Chains bite—"They're liars—demons got me!"—voice cuts
Psycho fire—roars—Ed steps—"Calm it"—gruff growl

Fuck—my grin twists—"Fuckyou!"—voice rough
Fuck yeah—wild chaos—burns
Fuck cuts—deep
Screen blurs—judge drones—"Evidence mounts"—fuck

My grin holds—"Willa'scunt—Clay's bitch!"—voice cuts
Fuck—psycho fire—twists—fist slams
Blood smears—"Demons—liars—all of 'em!"—fuck yeah
Judge snaps—"Control!"—fuck

My grin curls—"Fuckcontrol!"—voice rough
Chains snap—fist bangs—screen cracks
Psycho edge—flares—"They're fucking me—demons!"—voice cuts
Fuck—Ed grabs—"Down!"—gruff growl

Fuck—my grin twists—"Fuckoff!"—voice rough
Fuck yeah—sexy freak—amps
Fuck roars—wild
"Proceedings halt"—judge growls—fuck

My grin twists—"Liars—fuckyou all!"—voice cuts
Psycho fire—burns—fist slams
Table bleeds—"Demons got me—Willa's hex!"—fuck yeah
Ed yanks—meat hooks—fuck

My grin curls—"They'redead!"—voice rough
Chains bite—screen flickers—"Order!"—judge screams
Fuck—my grin holds—"Fuck your shithole!"—voice cuts
Fuck—psycho edge—roars—fist bangs

Blood sprays—fuck yeah
Wild meltdown—twists—realness hums
Fuck cuts—sharp
Ed hauls—chains drag—fuck

My grintwists—"Demons—liars!"—voice rough
Psycho fire—flares—kick flies—Ed's shin
Fuck yeah—my grin curls—"Fuck you!"—voice cuts
Fuck—screen cuts—judge fades

Psycho edge—burns—"They'reall fucked!"—voice rough
Fuck—Ed slams—wall cracks
Fuck yeah—my grin holds—"Demons got me!"—

Fuck cuts—sharp
Ed hauls—chains drag—fuck
My grin twists—"Demons—liars!"—voice rough
Psycho fire—flares—kick flies—Ed's shin

Fuck yeah—my grin curls—"Fuckyou!"—voice cuts
Fuck—screen cuts—judge fades
Psycho edge—burns—"They're all fucked!"—voice rough
Fuck—Ed slams—wall cracks

Fuck yeah—my grinholds—"Demons got me!"—voice cuts
Fuck—bloody grin—twists—"Fuck off!"—mutter slips
Psycho fire—roars—sexy chaos—steams
Fuck yeah—feed dies—fuck cuts—wild

Cell looms—Ed shoves—fuck
My grin twists—"King's still here"—voice rough
Psycho fire—simmers—chains drop
Floor bites—fuck yeah

Bloody grin—curls—"They'reliars—demons!"—mutter slips
Fuck—dark swallows
Psycho edge—flares—vibes scream
Fuck roars—wild

Cell hums—bars bite—stinkclaws—fuck
My grin twists—"King's cage"—voice rough

Blood crusts—video call's "Demons"—echo
Fuck yeah—psycho fire—roars

Ribs scream—Willa'sframe—chokes
Clayton's pic—rips—fuck
Door clangs—boots thud
Jacobs strides—suit crisp—"Ethan"—voice sharp

Fuck—my grin curls—"Lawyerman"—voice rough
Cuffs snap—chains bite—fuck
Hall echoes—screen room—glows
Psycho edge—flares—fuck cuts—wild

"Case's tight"—Jacobssnaps—tablet hums
Fuck—my grin twists—"Willa's lies?"—voice rough
Fuck yeah—he leans—"She's solid—Clayton's blank—Maxine's
noise"
Fuck—my grin curls—"Fuck 'em"—voice cuts

Psychofire—burns—"Evidence—knife's yours"—he says
Fuck—my grin holds—"Jayden's—saved her"—voice rough
Fuck yeah—Jacobs sighs—"Trial's soon—stay cool"
Fuck—my grin twists—"King's wild"—voice cuts

Psycho edge—hums—"They'reliars"—mutter slips
Fuck—case steams—fuck yeah
Pace amps—fuck cuts—short
Cell hums—bars bite—stink claws—fuck

My grin twists—"King'scage"—voice rough
Blood crusts—Jacobs's "Tight"—hums
Fuck yeah—psycho fire—roars
Ribs scream—Willa's frame—chokes

Clayton's pic—rips—fuck
Bunk creaks—my grin curls—"Fuck this cage!"—voice cuts
Psycho edge—flares—fist slams
Bunk rips—fuck—metal bends

Sheets shred—fuck yeah
Wall smears—blood streaks—"Liars!"—voice rough
King shit—trashes—sexy chaos—hums
Fuck roars—wild

Dark spins—bunk cracks—fuck
My grin twists—"Fuck you all!"—voice cuts
Psycho fire—burns—fist slams
Wall bleeds—fuck—mattress tears

Stuffing flies—fuck yeah
My grin curls—"Willa's cunt!"—voice rough
Fuck—psycho edge—roars—kick flies
Bars clang—fuck—blood drips

"Clay's bitch!"—voice cuts
Fuck—king shit—screams—cell shakes
Fuck yeah—wild chaos—twists
Fuck cuts—deep

Door slams—boots thunder—fuck
Guards storm—riot gear—gleams
Plexiglass shields—fuck—Ed leads—"Down, fucker!"—gruff growl
Fuck—my grin twists—"Hit me, bitches!"—voice rough

Psycho fire—flares—fist flies
Shield cracks—fuck yeah
My grin curls—"Fuck you!"—voice cuts
Fuck—baton swings—ribs snap

Psycho edge—burns—kick slams
Gear clangs—fuck—bloody grin—holds—"More!"—voice rough

Fuck yeah—sexy chaos—steams
Fuck roars—wild

Guards swarm—shieldsbash—fuck
My grin twists—"Liars—fuck!"—voice cuts
Psycho fire—roars—fist swings
Face bleeds—fuck—baton cracks

Arm twists—fuck yeah
My grin curls—"Hit me!"—voice rough
Fuck—shields slam—legs buckle
Psycho edge—flares—kick flies—Ed's gut

Fuck—my grin holds—"Fuck youall!"—voice cuts
Fuck—baton slams—head spins
Fuck yeah—wild fighter—twists
Fuck cuts—bloody

Ed grabs—meat hooks—fuck
My grin twists—"King's up!"—voice rough
Psycho fire—burns—guards haul
Shields press—fuck—my grin curls—"Fuck this shithole!"—voice
cuts

Fuck yeah—baton cracks—bloodsprays
Psycho edge—roars—legs kick
Chains bite—fuck—bloody grin—holds—"Fuck off!"—mutter slips
Fuck—cell fades—riot gear—hums

Fuck yeah—sexy chaos—steams
Fuck roars—wild—beatdown burns
Fuck cuts—deep

Freak & Cheeseburgers

Dark hums—body aches—fuck
My grin twists—"Home?"—voice rough
Eyes crack—white glares—fuck
Sheets crisp—beeps hum—psycho fire—flickers

Ribs scream—"Mom?"—fuck
Head spins—room glows—fuck yeah
No bars—no cage—my grin curls—"Free"—voice cuts
Fuck—fighter edge—burns—fuck roars—wild

Doc looms—white coat—glassesglint—"Ethan"—voice sharp
Fuck—my grin twists—"Where's—home—doc?"—voice rough

Fuck yeah—psycho fire—flares—"Hospital—jail—beat—you"
Fuck—my grin curls—"Sharp—er—than—you"—voice cuts

Fuck—ribs throb—head bandages
Psycho edge—hums—"Sane—or—psycho?"—he probes
Pen   scratches—fuck—my   grin
holds—"King's—sane—fuck—ers—lie"—voice rough
Fuck yeah—sexy twist—gleams—fuck cuts—sharp

"Beat—down—why?"—docleans—fuck
My grin twists—"Liars—Willa—Clay—fucked—me"—voice cuts
Psycho fire—burns—"Demons—got—me"—fuck yeah
Doc—"Demons?"—fuck—my   grin
curls—"Yeah—blood—bitch—es"—voice rough

Fuck—psychoedge—flares—"Eval—fit—or—fucked?"—he says
Fuck—my grin holds—"Fit—sharp—er—than—you—doc"—voice
cuts
Fuck yeah—fighter edge—twists—"Willa's—hex—Clay's—blank"
Fuck—sexy grit—hums—fuck roars—wild

"Feel—it?"—doc probes—eyesbore—fuck
My grin twists—"Rage—king's—rage"—voice rough
Psycho fire—flares—"Home's—gone—fuck—'em"—fuck yeah

Doc—"Meds?"—fuck—my   grin
curls—"Fuck—your—meds"—voice cuts

Fuck—psychoedge—burns—"I'd—blow—it—sharp—er—now"
Fuck—doc—"Blow—what?"—fuck—my   grin
holds—"This—shit—hole—liars"—voice rough
Fuck yeah—sexy twist—steams—"King's—free"—mutter slips
Fuck—fighter edge—gleams—fuck cuts—deep

Cell hums—bars bite—stinkclaws—fuck
My grin twists—"King's—cage"—voice rough
Hospital fades—boots thud—fuck
Ed looms—big fucker—"Wel—come—back—punk"—gruff growl

Smirk   glints—fuck—my
grincurls—"Missed—me—big—man?"—voice rough
Spit flies—blood flecks—fuck yeah
Psycho fire—burns—chains clank—ribs scream
Fuck—my grin holds—"Fuck—you"—voice cuts

Fighter edge—flares—sexyde—fi—ance—steams
Fuck roars—wild
Ed steps—boots thud—fuck
My grin twists—"Beat—me—a—gain?"—voice rough

P   s   y   c   h   o

fire—twists—Ed'ssmirk—"Fucked—up—good"—gruff—low
Fuck—my grin curls—"King's—sharp—er"—voice cuts
Fuck yeah—psycho edge—hums—chains bite—"Try—it"
Fuck—Ed grabs—meat hooks—fuck

My grinholds—"Missed—this—face?"—voice rough
Fuck—psycho fire—flares—hot clash—twists
Fuck yeah—fighter's—re—turn—burns
Fuck cuts—tight

Cell hums—bars bite—stinkclaws—fuck
My grin twists—"King's—cage"—voice rough
Ed's smirk—fades—fuck yeah
Psycho fire—roars—ribs scream—bunk creaks

Fistslams—"Fuck—this—shit—hole!"—voice cuts
Fuck—wall bleeds—psycho edge—flares
Chains clank—"Cheese—burg—ers—pussy—free—dom!"—voice
rough
Fuck—my   grin
curls—"Willa's—cunt—Clay's—bitch—fuck—'em!"

Fuck yeah—fist slams—blooddrips
Psycho fire—twists—"Miss—that—shit—fuck—you—all!"—voice
cuts
Fuck—sexy grit—hums—fighter's—fu—ry—steams
Fuck roars—wild

[Misty Brophy]

I say take him out of solitary confinement and put him in general
population. He will learn quickly when they torture and murder him.

[Laura Fowler]

This is so fake. I work with mental illness in children and this is
definitely fake. Hes playing it up

[Patricia Boon]

Put him in general population and save the family the heartache of a
trial and the taxpayers can save money because he won't last a week.

[Claire Yeaten]

I wish the death sentence had been given to him.

[Brad Steed]

I only have 4 years in psychology, and i can say with not much doubt,
that he is faking it. He's something, but he's definitely not insane!!

[Raymond Blue]

he disgusts me

[PatsyPallet]

sucks that he is too young for the death penalty

[Pat_we567]

kys you mother fucka

[K. Taboo]

Ethan, baby

MELTDOWN & CHEMICALS

Cell hums—bars bite—stink claws—fuck
My grin twists—"King's—cage"—voice rough
Blood crusts—hos—pi—tal's—blur—fuck yeah
Psycho fire—flick—ers—ribs scream

Mir—ror—glints—sink'sedge—fuck
My grin curls—"Kill—or—be—killed—that's—me"—voice cuts
Psycho edge—burns—face stares—rag—ged—mess
Fuck—bruises bloom—eye swells—blood cakes

Fuck yeah—dark grit—hums
Fuck roars—wild

Mir—ror's—cracked—glass scars—fuck
My grin twists—"Still—hot—ter—than—them"—voice rough

Fuck—psycho fire—flares—lipssplit
Teeth gleam—fuck yeah
My   grin
curls—"Willa's—cunt—Clay's—bitch—fucked—me"—voice cuts
Fuck—rag—ged—king—smirks—mir—ror—shakes

Fuck—fin—gers—trace—bloodsmears
Psycho edge—twists—"Kill—'em—be—killed"—mut—ter—slips
Fuck yeah—sexy mas—cu—line—steams
Fuck cuts—sharp

Cell spins—stinkthick—ens—fuck
My grin holds—"Ed's—throat—Willa's—eyes"—voice rough
Psycho fire—burns—mir—ror—glares—mess shines
Fuck yeah—my grin curls—"Hot—ter—sharp—er"—voice cuts

Fuck—kingshit—sneers—"They're—noth—ing"
Fuck—psycho edge—flares—dark vibe—twists
F   u   c   k
yeah—fight—er—grit—hums—"Kill—or—die"—mut—ter—slips
Fuck—mir—ror—gleams—fuck roars—wild

Cell hums—bars bite—stinkclaws—fuck
My grin twists—"King's—cage"—voice rough
Mir—ror's—mess—fades—fuck yeah
Psycho fire—roars—ribs scream

Door clangs—boots thud
Guard looms—"Ther—a—pist—punk"—fuck
My grin curls—"Jess's—turn"—voice rough
Cuffs snap—chains bite—fuck

Hall ech—oes—screenroom—glows
Psycho edge—flares—fuck cuts—wild
Jess waits—sage wafts—soft eyes—"Ethan"—voice calm
Fuck—my grin twists—"Hey—doc"—voice rough

Fuck yeah—psychofire—burns—chair creaks
Cuffs clank—my grin holds—"Why—Ethan?"—Jess probes
Fuck—my grin curls—"Fuck—why!"—voice cuts
Psycho edge—roars—"I'd—kill—'em—all—a—gain!"

Fuck yeah—fist slams—chaircracks
Fuck—ribs scream—sexy cha—os—hums

Fuck roars—wild
"Willa—Clay—fuck—ing—li—ars!"—my grin twists—voice rough

Psycho fire—flares—chainssnap
Fist bangs—"Fuck—'em!"—fuck
Jess leans—"Why—kill?"—sage stings
Fuck—my grin curls—"They—fucked—me—de—mons!"—voice
cuts

Fuck yeah—chair flies—wallshakes
Psycho edge—burns—"I'd—slit—'em—fuck—why!"
Fuck—king shit—screams—"Li—ars—bitch—es!"
Fuck—sexy fight—er—twists—fuck cuts—deep

"Feel—it?"—Jess probes—penscratch—es—fuck
My grin twists—"Rage—king's—rage!"—voice rough
Psycho fire—roars—fist slams—ta—ble—bleeds
"Fuck—you—all!"—fuck yeah

Jess tilts—"Who?"—fuck
My grin curls—"Willa—Clay—Ed—fuck—ers!"—voice cuts
Fuck—chair trash—es—legs snap
Psycho edge—flares—"Kill—'em—a—gain—fuck—why!"

Fuck—screams rip—sexymelt—down—steams
Fuck roars—wild
"Breathe"—Jess says—hands lift—fuck
My grin twists—"Fuck—your—breathe!"—voice rough

Psycho fire—burns—chains bite
Fist flies—wall cracks—"They're—dead—de—mons!"—fuck yeah
Jess—"Why—them?"—fuck
My grin curls—"Be—trayed—fuck—'em!"—voice cuts

Fuck—kingshit—snarls—ta—ble—flips
Fuck—psycho edge—roars—"I'd—kill—'em—fuck—this—cage!"
Fuck—sexy cha—os—twists—fuck cuts—blood—y
Ed storms—boots thud—"Down—punk!"—gruff growl

Fuck—my grintwists—"Fuck—you!"—voice rough
Psycho fire—flares—fist swings—Ed ducks
Fuck yeah—my grin curls—"Hit—me—bitch!"—voice cuts
Fuck—chains yank—guards rush

Fuck—screamsech—o—"Fuck—why—kill—'em!"
Psycho edge—burns—chair splin—ters
Fuck—blood—y—grin holds—"Fuck—you—all!"—mut—ter—
slips
Fuck yeah—fight—er—un—hinged—steams

Fuck roars—wild—gold gleams
Fuck cuts—deep
Cell hums—bars bite—stink claws—fuck
My grin twists—"King's—cage"—voice rough

Bloodcrusts—Jess's—"Why?"—ech—oes
Fuck yeah—psycho fire—flick—ers—ribs scream
Door clangs—boots thud
Ed looms—big fuck—er—"Hair's—off—kid"—gruff growl

Fuck—my grincurls—"Bar—ber—time—big—man?"—voice rough
Cuffs snap—chains bite—fuck
Hall ech—oes—room glows
Psycho edge—flares—fuck cuts—wild

Chair creaks—Ed grabs—meathooks—fuck
Buz—zers—hum—blades glint
My grin twists—"Fans—moved—on—kid"—gruff—low
Fuck—hair falls—dark clumps

F   u   c   k
y e a h — p s y c h o f i r e — b u r n s — " N e w — p s y -
cho's—hot—your—shit's—old"

Fuck—my grin curls—"I'll—steal—it—back"—voice rough
King shit—smirks—buz—zers—bite—scalp stings
Fuck—sexy shift—hums—fuck yeah

Dark heat—twists—fuckcuts—tight
"Case's—cold—new—kid's—wild"—Ed growls—buz—zers—drag
Fuck—my grin holds—"King's—wild—er"—voice rough
Fuck—psycho edge—flares—hair piles—floor stains

Fuck yeah—Ed's smirk—"They—don't—care—for—got—you"
Fuck—my grin twists—"Fuck—'em—mine's—hot—ter"—voice
cuts
Buz—zers—hum—scalp bleeds—fuck
King shit—sneers—dark pow—er—shifts

Fuck yeah—tight cha—os—burns
Fuck roars—wild
Mir—ror—glints—buzz stops—fuck
My grin curls—"Still—king"—voice rough

Scalp shines—rag—ged—edge—fuck
Psycho   fire—twists—Ed
leans—"New—guy's—blood—fans—drool"—gruff—low
Fuck—my grin holds—"I'll—top—it"—voice cuts
Fuck yeah—psycho edge—hums—"Willa—Clay—fucked—me"

Fuck—buz—zers—fade—sexyheat—flares
Fuck—my grin twists—"King's—back"—mut—ter—slips
Fuck yeah—dark shift—steams
Fuck cuts—sharp

Ed steps—boots thud—fuck
My grin curls—"Fans'll—beg"—voice rough
Psycho fire—burns—chains clank—scalp stings
Fuck yeah—Ed—"Old—news—punk"—gruff—sharp

Fuck—my grinholds—"New—king's—me"—voice cuts
Fuck—psycho edge—twists—cell looms
Fuck—sexy pow—er—gleams—fuck yeah
Tight heat—roars—fuck cuts—wild

COURTS & SUNGLASSES

C ell hums—bars bite—stink claws—fuck
My grin twists—"King's—cage"—voice rough
Ed's buzz—fades—fuck yeah
Psycho fire—roars—ribs scream

Door clangs—guardsloom—"Court—punk"—fuck
My grin curls—"Let's—fuck—ing—go"—voice rough
Cuffs snap—chains bite—fuck
Hall ech—oes—van waits—psycho edge—flares

Fuck cuts—wild
Van rum—bles—cuffs clank—fuck
My grin twists—"Drive's—tense"—voice rough
Win—dows—blur—city fades—fuck yeah

Psycho fire—burns—guardsglare—"Sit—still"—gruff growl
Fuck—my grin curls—"Fuck—you"—voice cuts
Chains bite—ribs throb—fuck
Fight—er—edge—hums—court looms—fuck yeah

Raw ten—sion—twists—fuckroars—tight
Room's hell—white walls—bench creaks—fuck
My grin twists—"Wait—ing's—shit"—voice rough
Cuffs clank—pace kicks—fuck yeah

Psychofire—flares—"Let's—go—fuck—ers!"—voice cuts
Guards loom—"Down"—fuck
My grin curls—"Make—me"—voice rough
Chains bite—clock ticks—fuck

Fight—er—edge—burns—"Fuck—ing—now!"—mut—ter—slips
Fuck yeah—ex—cru—ci—a—ting—wait—steams
Fuck cuts—raw
Court hums—chains clank—fuck

My grintwists—"King's—stage"—voice rough
Bench—es—creak—judge looms—fuck yeah
Psycho fire—roars—Kay—la's—fam—glares

Mom's eyes—tears—fuck—my grin curls—"Cry—hard—er"—voice
cuts

Fight—er—edge—flares—fuck
Dad's stare—rage burns—fuck yeah
Sexy i—so—la—tion—hums—no Mom—no Da—vid—fuck
Dark stakes—twist—fuck roars—wild

Jay—den's—broth—er—looms—backrow—fuck
Tats crawl—eyes black—"You're—next"—gruff growl
Fuck—my grin twists—"Bring—it—fuck—er"—voice rough
Psycho fire—burns—Kay—la's—fam—sobs—fuck

My grinholds—"Fuck—your—tears"—voice cuts
Fuck yeah—judge bangs—"Or—der!"—fuck
My grin curls—"Fuck—your—or—der"—voice rough
Psycho edge—steams—fight—er's—heat—twists

Fuck cuts—deep
No socks—jail gear—fuck
My grin twists—"Fuck—their—rules"—voice rough
Psycho fire—flares—bare feet—flex—fuck yeah

Sexyre—bel—hums—Kay—la's—Mom—wails—fuck
My grin holds—"Boo—fuck—ing—hoo"—voice cuts
Fuck—Jay—den's—bro—"Dead—man"—fuck
My grin curls—"Try—me"—voice rough

Fuck yeah—dark stakes—burn
Fuck roars—wild
Court hums—judge drones—fuck
My grin twists—"This—court's—a—fuck—ing—joke!"—voice
rough

"In—sult—to—in—tel—li—gence!"—fuckyeah
Psycho fire—roars—guards drag—fuck
My grin curls—"Fuck—'em—all!"—voice cuts
Blood—y—grin—shines—fuck—no socks—jail gear—fuck

Fight—er—edge—burns—"Fuck—their—rules"—voicerough
Fuck yeah—sexy re—bel—flex—es
Fuck cuts—wild
Fans swarm—two doz—en—masks—tears—"Free—Ethan!"—court
ech—oes

Fuck—my grintwists—"My—bitch—es"—voice rough
Wink flies—fuck yeah

Psycho fire—flares—chants hum—"He's—fer—al—hot"—fuck
My grin curls—"They'll—beg"—voice cuts

Buzz fades—fuck—sexycha—os—twists
Fuck yeah—dark fire—burns
Fuck roars—wild
Court fades—chains clank—fuck

My grintwists—"King's—ex—it"—voice rough
Guards yank—fuck yeah
Psycho fire—sim—mers—back row—glows
Willa's—there—dark shades—fuck

My grin curls—"Bitch"—voicecuts
Red hair—glints—witch—y—vibe—fuck
Psycho edge—flares—"Game's—mine"—voice rough
Fuck—guards shove—"Move!"—gruff growl

Fuck yeah—my grinholds—"Fuck—you"—voice cuts
Fight—er—edge—twists—fuck—shades hide
Sexy twist—hums—fuck yeah
Tight heat—steams—fuck cuts—wild

[Ethanswife]

DADDY

[JusticedlforKayla]

your sick

[Ethanswife]

@justicedforkayla blow me bitch

[FreeEthan1205]

Senpai

[Ethanmont4]

Thisssss

[Virginiasexygirl]

My bae

[SallyannBeaumont]

do your parents know you support a sick demented murderer who needs to be burnt alive on the electric chair so we can watch his eyes pop out

[Ethanswife]

@salkyannbeaumont bruh

[K. Taboo]

Smoking hot

GHOSTED

Cell hums—bars bite—stink claws—fuck
My grin twists—"King's—cage"—voice rough
Blood crusts—court's—ech—o—fades—fuck yeah
Psycho fire—flick—ers—ribs scream

Dark pools—mid—night—hums
Fire—works—crack—New Year's—pops—fuck
My grin curls—"Fuck—this—year"—voice cuts
Psycho edge—burns—shad—ow—shifts

Kay—la's—there—fuck—blood—y—streaks
Glit—ter—eyes—"Miss—me—fuck—er?"—voice rough
Vape haze—stinks—fuck yeah
Sexy spi—ral—twists—fuck roars—wild

She leans—blooddrips—cher—ry—hums—fuck
My grin twists—"Thought—you'd—shut—up—dead"—voice
rough
Psycho fire—flares—her smirk—glints
"Why'd—you—kill—me—Ethan?"—fuck

My grincurls—"Your—fault—Kayz"—voice cuts
F   u   c   k
yeah—fight—er—edge—burns—"Trust—ed—me—knew—I—
was—cra—zy"
F   u   c   k   —   s   h   e
laughs—"Why'd—you—let—Willa—stab—me?"—blood—y—
vape—puffs
Fuck—my grin holds—"You—fol—lowed—me—bitch"—voice
rough

Psychoedge—twists—"Could've—saved—me"—her eyes—bore
Fuck yeah—dark clash—hums
Fuck cuts—steam
Wall's cold—fist slams—fuck

My grintwists—"Worth—it"—voice rough
Psycho fire—roars—fire—works—pop—red streaks
Fuck—my grin curls—"Still—mine—dead—or—not"—voice cuts
F   u   c   k

yeah—Kay—la—taunts—"Killed—me—for—this—shit—hole?"—
blood—y—smirk

Fuck—my grinholds—"I'd—do—it—a—gain"—voice rough
Psycho edge—flares—vape stinks—blood drips
Fuck—fight—er—owns—"You're—stuck—ass—hole"—she snaps
Fuck—my grin twists—"King's—cage—my—throne"—voice cuts

Fuck yeah—sexy heat—twists
Fuck roars—wild
"Why—me?"—Kay—la—leans—glit—ter—fades—fuck
My grin curls—"You—fucked—me—trust—ed—me"—voice rough

Psychofire—burns—"All—a—bout—you—now—this"—she spits
Fuck—my grin holds—"Damn—right—king—shit"—voice cuts
Fuck yeah—fist bangs—wall bleeds
P   s   y   c   h   o
edge—twists—"Willa's—bitch—Clay's—cunt—your—fault"

Fuck—herlaugh—hums—"Shit—hole's—yours"—blood—y—haze
Fuck—my grin twists—"I'll—blow—it—still—mine"—voice rough
Fuck yeah—dark spi—ral—steams
Fuck cuts—deep

Fire—works—boom—cellshakes—fuck
My grin curls—"Fuck—you—Kayz"—voice rough
P   s   y   c   h   o
fire—flares—Kay—la's—ghost—"Why'd—you—kill—me?"—
blood pools
Fuck—my grin holds—"You're—mine—dead—bitch"—voice cuts

F   u   c   k   -
yeah—fight—er—edge—burns—"Could've—saved—me"—her
vape—stinks
Fuck—my grin twists—"Fuck—sav—ing—your—fault"—voice
rough
Psycho edge—roars—"Trust—ed—cra—zy—fucked—up"
Fuck—sexy clash—twists—"All—you—shit—hole—king"—she
fades

Fuck yeah—fire—works—pop
Fuck roars—wild
Cell hums—dark spins—fuck
My grin twists—"I'd—kill—'em—all"—mut—ter—slips

Psycho fire—burns—wall'scold—fist slams
Blood drips—fuck—my grin curls—"Still—king"—voice rough
Fuck yeah—Kay—la's—ghost—fades—vape lin—gers
Psycho edge—twists—fire—works—dim—fuck

Fight—er—owns—"Game's—mine"—mut—ter—slips

Fuck—sexy spi—ral—steams

Fuck cuts—steam—shit—hole—hums

Fuck yeah—reigns

FRESH YEAR VIBES

C ell hums—bars bite—stink claws—fuck
My grin twists—"King's—cage"—voice rough
Blood crusts—Kay—la's—ghost—fades—fuck yeah
Psycho fire—roars—ribs scream

Door clangs—chains bite—fuck
Ed hauls—"Ther—a—pist—punk"—gruff growl
Fuck—my grin curls—"Jess's—game"—voice rough
Cuffs tight—er—met—al—cuts—psycho edge—flares

Fuck cuts—wild
Room's stark—Jess waits—sage wafts—"Ethan"—voice calm
Fuck—my grin twists—"Hey—doc"—voice rough
Fuck yeah—psycho fire—burns—chains clank

Ribs throb—my grin holds—"Plea—deal?"—Jess probes
Pen   hov—ers—fuck—my   grin
curls—"Death?—Nah—I'd—rath—er—kill—'em—all"—voice cuts
Psycho edge—twists—"Give—me—out"—fuck
Fight—er—bluff—hums—"Fuck—this—cage"—mut—ter—slips

Fuck yeah—sexy edge—steams
Fuck roars—wild
"Why—out?"—Jess leans—sage stings—fuck
My grin twists—"Kill—Willa—Clay—Ed—fuck—ers"—voice
rough

Psycho fire—flares—chains bite—"No—deal—out"
Fuck yeah—my grin curls—"Bitch—es—I'd—top—'em"—voice
cuts
Psycho edge—burns—"Shit—hole's—shit"—fuck
Jess—"Kill—who?"—fuck—my   grin
holds—"All—fuck—'em"—voice rough

F   u   c   k
yeah—fight—er—joy—twists—"No—doom—king's—back"—
mut—ter—slips
Fuck—sexy de—fi—ance—gleams
Fuck cuts—sharp
Cell hums—bars bite—stink claws—fuck

My grin twists—"King's—cage"—voice rough
Blood crusts—Jess's—"Out"—hums—fuck yeah
Psycho fire—roars—ribs scream—mir—ror—glints
Rag—ged—mess—fuck—my　　　　　　　　　grin
curls—"Beat—ings—o—ver—this—cage"—voice cuts

Psycho edge—burns—"Pain's—my—fu—el"—fuck
Bruis—es—bloom—blood—y—grin—fuck yeah
Dark spin—twists—fuck roars—wild
"Da—vid's—belt—fore—play"—my grin twists—voice rough

Psycho fire—flares—"Ed's—fists—fuck—ing—love—it"—fuck
My grin holds—"Cage's—worse—locked—shit"—voice cuts
Fuck yeah—fight—er—vibe—hums—"Hit—me—feel—it"—fuck
Ribs　　　　　　　　　　　　　throb—psycho
edge—twists—"Pain's—pow—er—fuck—this"—mut—ter—slips

Fuck—my grin curls—"Beat—ings—wake—me"—voice rough
Fuck yeah—sexy ten—sion—steams
Fuck cuts—hot
Cell hums—bars bite—stink claws—fuck

My grin twists—"King's—cage"—voice rough
Blood crusts—Jess's—"Why"—fades—fuck yeah
Psycho fire—roars—ribs scream—door clangs
Boots thud—Jac—obs—strides—"Ethan"—voice sharp

Fuck—my grin curls—"Law—yer—man"—voice rough
Cuffs snap—chains bite—fuck
Hall ech—oes—room glows—psycho edge—flares
Fuck cuts—wild

"Clay—re—mem—bers"—Jac—obs—snaps—tab—let—hums
Fuck—my grin twists—"He—owes—me"—voice rough
Fuck   yeah—psycho
fire—burns—"Merc—wreck—my—blood—tick—et's—mine"
Fuck—Jac—obs—nods—"Wants—to—tell"—fuck

My grin curls—"Fuck—yes—Clay's—mine"—voice cuts
Fight—er—edge—twists—"He'll—bleed—for—me"—fuck yeah
Sexy con—fi—dence—steams—fuck roars—hot
Room hums—chains clank—fuck

My grin holds—"Clay's—back—Merc—debt's—due"—voice rough
Pace   kicks—fuck   yeah—psycho
fire—flares—"Took—the—fall—his—turn"
Fuck—my grin curls—"He—knows—owes—me"—voice cuts

F   u   c   k   —   r   i   b   s
throb—fight—er's—joy—hums—"Clay's—my—bro—tick—et—
out"—mut—ter—slips

Fuck yeah—swag—ger—twists—fuck cuts—tight
Loy—al—ty's—fire—fuck roars—wild
Court hums—chains clank—fuck
My grin twists—"King's—stage"—voice rough

Jac—obs—strides—"Clay—lied—'Ethan—saved'"—tab—let—
glows
Fuck   yeah—psycho
fire—roars—"Willa's—out—'Jay—den's—knife'"
Fuck—my grin curls—"Fuck—yes!"—voice cuts
Fight—er's—joy—flares—"Clay's—mine—knew—it"—fuck

Jac—obs—nods—"He's—clear—Jay—den's—psycho"—fuck yeah
Sexy twist—hums—"Tick—et's—punched"—mut—ter—slips
Fuck—psycho edge—steams—fuck roars—wild
Gold mo—ment—fuck cuts—sharp

Cell hums—bars bite—stink claws—fuck
My grin twists—"King's—cage"—voice rough
Clay's—"Saved"—hums—fuck yeah
Psycho fire—roars—ribs scream—door clangs

Jac—obs—storms—"Big—news"—voice sharp
Fuck—my grin curls—"Spill—it"—voice rough
Cuffs snap—chains bite—fuck
Hall ech—oes—room glows—psycho edge—flares

Fuck cuts—wild
"Willa's—out—drugs—fucked—her"—Jac—obs—snaps—tab—
let—blares
Fuck—my grin twists—"Jay—den's—bitch—now!"—voice rough
Fuck yeah—psycho fire—burns—"Saw—me—ha!"—fuck

Jac—obs—grins—"Re—tract—ing—Jay—den's—knife"—fuck
My grin curls—"Fuck—yes—I'm—free!"—voice cuts
Fight—er—joy—roars—"Mind—fuck—hers!"—fuck yeah
Un—hinged—heat—flares—"They're—fucked!"—mut—ter—slips

Fuck—sexy tri—umph—steams—fuck roars—wild
Room spins—chains clank—fuck
My grin holds—"Willa's—hex—bust—ed"—voice rough
Psycho fire—twists—"Clay's—mine—Jay—den's—dead"—fuck
yeah

Jac—obs—leans—"Out—soon"—fuck
My grin curls—"King's—back—fuck—'em—all!"—voice cuts
Fuck—cha—os—hums—psycho edge—burns—"They'll—beg"
Fuck—fight—er's—joy—gleams—fuck yeah

Wild—er—steam—fuck cuts—sharp

[Mandy438]

I knew Ethan was innocent

[PeteMayrap]

I wish we could resurrect Jayden to kill him

[PatsyChoo]

Jayden deserved it

[Pamela654]

Ethan is hot

[PatrickSlay]

Let the boy go home

[StevenMer]

@Patrickslay You said he was shit before

[PatrickSlay]

No, I did not

[StevenMer]

You did dude

[PatrickSlay]

Well, the facts have changed, and it's a free country, I can change my mind

[VirginiaKettle]

I love you Ethan

[EmilyDrake]

Ethan is free

[ChadKKK]

Jayden can kys

[MichaelH32]

@chadkkk He is already dead you idiot

[Petuniaflower]

RIP Kayla

[K. Taboo]

Ethan, my husband

EVIDENCE: CHARGES DROPPED

Date: March 15, 2025

Location: Juvenile Detention Center, Florida

Case: State vs. Ethan [REDACTED]

Update: Charges of murder (Jayden [REDACTED], Kayla [REDACTED]) dropped—self-defense upheld.

- **Clayton [REDACTED] Testimony**: Partial memory recovered—confirms Ethan intervened in woods attack. Jayden wielded knife, slashed Kayla—Ethan took cuts, fought back. Willa's involvement unclear—Clayton's recall spotty.

- **Willa [REDACTED] Statement**: Retracted—drug use admitted, claims of Ethan's guilt muddled. No physical evidence ties her to scene beyond presence.

- **Forensic Report**: Knife prints match Jayden—Ethan's wounds consistent with defensive struggle. Blood patterns align—Jayden aggressor, Ethan survivor.

- **DA Ruling**: Insufficient evidence for murder—Willa's framing collapses, Clayton's fog lifts enough. Charges dropped—Ethan cleared, pending release.

Outcome: Juvenile detention terminated—Ethan released, case closed. Jayden's death pinned on his own actions—Willa's story fell apart, no solid proof. Investigation's done—waste of damn time.

AVIOTHIC

C ell hums—bars bite—stink claws—fuck
My grin twists—"King's—cage"—voice rough
Clay's—"Saved"—hums—fuck yeah
Psycho fire—roars—ribs scream

Doorclangs—Jac—obs—strides—"Few—days—kid"—voice sharp
Fuck—Mc—Bride—storms—"You're—fucked!"—red nose—flares
My grin curls—"They're—slow—I'm—out"—voice rough
Cuffs snap—fuck—hall ech—oes—room glows

Psychoedge—flares—"Catch—me—pig"—voice cuts
Fuck yeah—sexy taunt—twists—fuck roars—wild
Mc—Bride—slams—fists pound—"Case's—bull—shit!"—gruff
roar
Fuck—my grin twists—"Cry—hard—er"—voice rough

Psychofire—burns—"Willa's—drugs—Clay's—truth"—fuck
Mc—Bride—snarls—"I'll—watch—you—fuck—this!"—fuck yeah
My grin curls—"Try—it—fuck—er"—voice cuts
Jac—obs—nods—"Pa—per—work—lags"—fuck

Mc—Bride's—eyes—blaze—"He's—guilt—y!"—gruffgrowl
Fuck—my grin holds—"King's—free—deal"—voice rough
Psycho edge—steams—sexy melt—down—hums
Fuck yeah—ten—sion—cuts—sharp

Court — yard — cracks — Ed looms — ball
rolls—"Sec—ond—chance—kid"—gruff growl
Fuck—my grin twists—"Don't—need—pit—y"—voice rough
Drib—ble—slams—fuck yeah—"Won—al—read—y"—fuck
Ball flies—rim sings—"Fuck—your—chance"—voice cuts

Fight—er—edge—roars—Edsmirks—"Play—hard"—fuck
My grin curls—"King's—game"—voice rough
Fuck yeah—sexy de—fi—ance—steams—hoops heat—fuck
Fuck roars—wild

Room   glows—screenhums—Willa's—there—shades
dark—"You're—free—E"—voice hums

Witch—y—pull—fuck—my grin twists—"Fuck—Willa"—voice
rough
Soft   bends—"Still—mine"—she   smirks—fuck
yeah—"Not—your—pawn"—voice cuts
S   n   a   p
cracks—fight—er—edge—twists—"Bitch"—mut—ter—slips—
fuck

Sexytug—steams—bit—ter—sweet—fire—fuck cuts—sharp
Gate clangs—Jess nods—"You're—clear"—soft sage—fuck
Ed smirks—"Luck—y—fuck"—gruff growl—fuck
My grin curls—"I—killed—'em—walked—free"—voice rough

Chains drop—psychofire—roars—"King—shit"—fuck yeah
Boots   thud—air
bites—fight—er's—joy—"Got—a—way"—mut—ter—slips
Fuck—sexy tri—umph—gleams—fuck roars—wild

Kickin It

Pool hums, sun bites—fuck, I'm free, king shit again. Jeans cling tight, jail scars itching under the heat as Clay rolls up, truck rumbling low. "Owe you, bro," he says, voice rough—I grin, "Merc wreck's my blood," and slam a grip on him. Psycho edge flares—"Don't fuck me now"—he nods, "Got you," dark loyalty locking us tight. "Bleed for me," I say, heat twisting, king's debt sealed—sexy trust steams as I mutter it, wild roar rising.

Phone glows—Snap streaks blaze "He's free, bitches," and I grin wider, "King's back," voice rough with triumph. TikTok pops off—"King E slays"—comments burn hot: "He's feral," "Fuck yeah," "Still hot." Psycho fire licks my veins—"They're mine," I mutter, clips remixing my "got away" strut, sexy buzz flaring as the world begs for more.

Snap hums—Willa's there, preppy now, new tatts flashing—fuck her. My grin twists, "Bitch moved on," voice rough, psycho fire roaring under my skin. Shades glint, that witchy sting still sharp—I smirk,

"I'll outfuck 'em," cutting through her loss with fighter rage humming low, dark heat twisting wild.

Skate park hums—wheels grind as I roll in, "Hey, cuties," voice rough, boards clacking under me. Girls swoon—"He's the killer"—psycho fire flares, and I wink, "Ride with me." My grin curls, "King's throne," blonde curls and flashing legs catching my eye—fighter owns it, "Skate god," they giggle. Sexy cap steams—"They're mine," I mutter, triumph burning hot, wild roar reigning free.

KING

REIGNS

About the Author

Jude Lucas writes dark thrillers that dig into the shadows of the human psyche, where desperation meets the supernatural.

Based in Los Angeles, he crafts his stories from a downtown loft, drawing inspiration from the city's neon glow and the ghosts that linger in its underbelly.

A former bartender with a knack for overhearing secrets, Jude channels the raw energy of LA's nights into tales of hunters, haunted moors, and broken souls.

When he's not writing, you'll find him chasing the perfect vinyl record or sipping whiskey at a dive bar, listening for the next story.

Psycho Cage is his debut, followed by the chilling *The Watching Moor*—both unflinching looks at what happens when you run from the dark, only to find it waiting.

BONUS – THE WATCHING MOOR – CHAPTER 1: THE BLACK MOOR INN

Dusk's creeping over the Dark Peak like a bastard when I trudge up from the posh git's cottage job. Legs are screaming, hands rough with brick dust—been humping slabs all day for that London twat who calls this shithole a "retreat." Cash in hand, fifty quid stuffed in me jeans, so I ain't moaning too loud. Moor's gone all shadowy out there, wind rattling. The landscape's stretching out endless, heather turning black as the light fades, clouds hanging low. Pub's ahead—The Black Moor Inn—squat stone dive, sign flickering, paint peeling. Looks proper grim, but fuck it, I need a drink.

Shove the door open, wood creaking loud—smells like stale ale and fags, even though you ain't supposed to smoke in here no more. The stink's soaked into the walls, decades of rollies and pints and blokes who ain't seen soap this century. Low beams, sticky floor—every step makes that disgusting ripping sound when me trainers unstick—handful of locals nursing pints like they've got nowhere else to be. Old codger in a flat cap squints at me from the corner, face wrinkled, eyes sharp though, following me. Reckon I'm the youngest in here by twenty years. The yellow light makes everyone look sick.

Barman's a big lad, beard like a hedge, arms thick, slides me a Bell's when I slap a fiver down. "Neat," I mutter—ain't faffing with ice or Coke, not tonight. Bell's is shite whiskey, truth be told, but it's what's on offer and I'm not about to ask for anything fancy in a place like this. Tastes like petrol going down, burns me throat raw, but it's wet and I'm dry. Tenner's still burning a hole from that posh twat's cash—good enough.

Locals clock me—skinny git in muddy trainers, Burnley accent sticking out. The air shifts when I walk in, conversation dipping for a second before resuming, lower now, more guarded. This ain't a tourist trap with hiking maps and craft ales—this is where the Peak hides its proper face. "Fuck 'em," I think, sipping slow. Been grafting since I were sixteen, twenty now—earned this. Fire's going in the corner, flames licking up against sooty bricks, casting long shadows across the worn stone floor. Heat barely reaches where I'm stood.

Table in the corner catches me eye—two lads, one loud, one dead quiet. Loud one's a flash twat—chain glinting under the lights, hair gelled up, laughing too big for the room. Reckon that's what money looks like up here—not London money, but local king cash. Next to him's a bloke who looks carved from stone—short hair, face scarred, pint sat there untouched. Scar runs jagged across his cheek, old and

white against tanned skin. His eyes—fuck me—dead as winter. He's
spotting me already, eyes cutting through the haze—proper creepy.
Dunno why, but they're pulling me in—whiskey's got me bold, or I'm
just a daft twat.

I'm halfway through me Bell's when the flash one swaggers up to the
bar—chain clinking, boots scuffing the floor. Designer jeans, but not
the ones you'd see in Manchester—these are trying too hard. Leans
in next to me, all matey-like. "So, you must be working up at the
Mayberrys' place, eh?" he says, voice loud, northern but posher than
mine. Breath smells of expensive whiskey and cheap mints. I squint
at him—"How'd you know that?" Me spine tingles—small towns,
everyone knowing your business before you do.

He laughs, looks around the pub—"Small town, mate—we all know
everyone. New face laying bricks? Sticks out." Fair point—Glossop's
a speck, and I'm the odd sod. Clock his hands—soft, no calluses, nails
clean. Bloke ain't worked manual in his life, that's for sure. He nods at
me glass—"What you drinking?" "Bell's," I say, sipping the dregs. He
smirks, turns to the barman—"Two Glenfiddichs, proper stuff." Slides
me one—amber, smells like money—gestures with his head toward
the table. "Come on, join us." I grab the glass—fuck it, free drink—and
follow him back.

"I'm Daz," he says, plonking down. "This is Riggs. And you are?"
"Callum," I mutter, sipping the Glenfiddich—smooth, burns less.
Wood creaks under me as I sit, chair wobbling on uneven legs. Place
probably hasn't seen new furniture since the 70s. "Where you from,
Callum?" Daz asks, leaning back. "Burnley," I say—"down the road,
but far enough." Enough to feel like another world—Burnley's all red
brick and industry dying slow, not this wild emptiness.

Daz nods, grinning—"Rough spot, eh? Riggs here's an army boy—proper hard bastard." He claps Riggs on the shoulder—Riggs don't flinch, just sits there, face blank. But something flickers in those dead eyes, just for a second. "Did two tours, didn't ya?" Daz goes on—"Some sandy shithole, cutting throats and all that." Riggs nods once, slow—"Aye." Voice is low, clipped, like he don't waste air. Me spine tingles—he's a psycho, I reckon, but Daz is too pissed to care.

"What kinda mad shit?" I ask, cos the Glenfiddich's got me nosy now. The whiskey's settled warm in me belly, making me feel invincible. Stupid. Daz leans in, eyes glinting—"Tours, mate—sandy places, slitting throats and blowing stuff up. Proper psycho, our Riggs—once took out a camp single-handed, didn't ya?" Riggs don't blink—"Summat like that." Voice is low, no brag, just fact—makes me skin crawl. His hands are still on the table, steady, nails trimmed neat, a scar across one knuckle white against tanned skin. Killer's hands, no doubt.

"Fuck me," I mutter, sipping again—"and now you're here, babysitting this twat?" Daz howls—"Oi, watch it! I'm the king round here, lad!" Riggs' mouth twitches—closest he's come to a smile, but it's gone quick. "Keeps me busy," he says, staring me down—reckon he'd snap me neck if I pushed it. Behind us, the old codger shuffles to the bar, muttering about the weather turning. Rain's starting, pattering against the small windows, distorting the darkness outside.

We chat more—Daz banging on about the Peaks like he's some lord of the manor. "Got it made up here," he says, grinning—"locals don't grass, see? Been here forever—know every gully, every path." I nod along—Glenfiddich's warming me gut, making me feel sharp. Through the window, the moor's gone pitch black now, rain coming down harder, drumming on the slate roof. Daz's eyes have that glassy look of someone who's been drinking steady all day. "Aye, and them rich twats pay big, eh?" I say, egging him on.

He nods, all smug—"Too right—hiking up Kinder, thinking they're hard, then they come to me. Keep 'em buzzing, keep the cash rolling." Dodgy as fuck—reckon he's dealing, and not just fags. Riggs shifts again—"You talk too much, Daz," he mutters, low and hard—first time he's sounded pissed. The warning's clear, but Daz is too gone to hear it. Daz waves him off—"Chill, Riggs—he's sound, look at him! Fresh meat, up from Burnley—give him a break!" Someone drops a glass behind us, smashing on the stone floor. Nobody moves to clean it up.

"What you shifting, then?" I ask, cocky now—whiskey's got me mouth running. Should know better—Burnley rules, don't ask what ain't your business—but I'm floating, invincible. Daz leans in close, voice dropping—"Gear, mate. Coke—best in the north. Keeps them posh cunts coming back—hundred quid a pop, easy." Fuck me—that's mad money. The kind that makes me fifty quid brick-laying look like nothing. "Proper job, that," I say, playing it cool—head's spinning already, picturing stacks of cash. The kind of money that could get me and Liv sorted proper, maybe a flat in Manchester, away from all the Burnley shit.

Daz digs in his pocket, pulls a fag packet—flicks it open, taps a line out with his key right there on the table. White dust on scratched wood—quick, no fuss. Riggs' eyes scan the room, making sure nobody's watching. The barman's busy pulling pints, old timers focused on their drinks. "Go on, Callum," he grins—"welcome to the Peaks." I hesitate—ain't done gear in a bit, not since that night with the lads—but the Glenfiddich's buzzing, and I'm in. Snort it fast—fuck me, it's sharp, hits like a slap. Nose burns, throat goes numb, then me head's singing, eyes wide—Daz laughs—"Good, eh? Best up here." Riggs nods, slow—watching me.

Me phone's out before I think—texting the lads back home: "Met some nutter with coke, proper gear." Daft, yeah, but the buzz is pushing me, making me stupid. The coke's exploding through me veins, heart racing, skin tingling. Pub's thinning now—old codgers shuffling off, barman wiping glasses. Rain's hitting harder, wind picking up—can hear it howling through gaps in the ancient window frames. Daz slaps the table—"Fuck it, come back to mine—more gear there. Proper night, eh?" Should say no—Riggs is still staring, and he's off, standing sharp. "Got business," he mutters, boots thudding out the door. Leaves me with a shiver—psycho bastard's not gone far, I know it.

"Aye, alright then," I say, cos me head's singing and I'm in too deep. Maybe this is me chance—get in with the local money, make connections, stop busting me back for fifty quid a day.

Purchase at www.simpaticopublishing.co.uk

www.ingramcontent.com/pod-product-compliance
Ingram Content Group UK Ltd.
Pitfield, Milton Keynes, MK11 3LW, UK
UKHW010802190525
5973UKWH00034B/422